Vicki Blum

A Gathering of Unicorns

Cover by
Mark Thurman

Illustrated by
Julie Rocheleau

Vicki Blum

A Gathering
of
Unicorns

Cover by
Mark Thurman

Illustrated by
Julie Rocheleau

Scholastic Canada Ltd.

Toronto New York London Auckland Sydney
Mexico City New Delhi Hong Kong Buenos Aires

Scholastic Canada Ltd.
175 Hillmount Road, Markham, Ontario L6C 1Z7, Canada

Scholastic Inc.
555 Broadway, New York, NY 10012, USA

Scholastic Australia Pty Limited
PO Box 579, Gosford, NSW 2250, Australia

Scholastic New Zealand Limited
Private Bag 94407, Greenmount, Auckland, New Zealand

Scholastic Ltd.
Villiers House, Clarendon Avenue, Leamington Spa,
Warwickshire CV32 5PR, UK

Map by Paul Heersink/Paperglyphs

Edited by Laura Peetoom

National Library of Canada Cataloguing in Publication

Blum, Vicki, 1955-
A gathering of unicorns / Vicki Blum ; illustrated by Julie Rocheleau.

ISBN 0-439-97417-8

I. Rocheleau, Julie II. Title.

PS8553.L86G38 2003   jC813'.54   C2003-901068-6
                            PZ7

6 5 4 3 2 1   Printed in Canada   03 04 05 06 07

To Linda and Lori,
mes soeurs extraordinaires

"When thou goest out to battle against
thine enemies, and seest horses, and chariots,
and a people more than thou, be not afraid . . . "
Deuteronomy 20:1

North Bundelag & its Neighbouring Lands

Dragon Island

Unicorn Valley

Ogre Forest

North Bundelag

Elf Village

Fairy Village

Ice-Fields

The Black Badlands

River

The Battleground

River of Songs

South Bundelag

Elf Village

Raden's Mine

Entrance from Earth

Chapter 1

Arica looked up from her math test to see an elf standing in the classroom doorway.

It wasn't a pretty elf like the ones found in story-books — small and slender, with locks of cornsilk hair, delicate pointed ears, and dimpled cheeks. This elf had a thatch of brown hair that sprang out like the bristles of an old brush, huge floppy ears half-covered by an ugly hat, and a short, rain-barrel body. But that wasn't the worst of it. The poor thing was badly in need of a good scrubbing. His clothing was wrinkled and grimy, and a smear of half-dried mud ran from his brow to his chin.

She knew it was Nue right away. But that was

impossible. He was in Bundelag, where he had gone after helping to bring her kidnapped mother home. However, Arica had learned that when it came to the magical land of Bundelag, almost anything was possible — ever since she had fallen through the crack in her Grandmother's kitchen floor and ended up there herself. So this must be Nue — here to give her an important message. Convinced that this was the case, she leaped from her desk and rushed up the aisle.

"Arica!" her teacher's voice barked, bringing her skidding to a halt. "Where are you going?"

Arica stared helplessly at her teacher's frowning face and wondered how to explain why she had left her seat without permission. Lying was not an option, but she couldn't tell the truth either. And she had to keep everyone's attention away from the door. If her teacher or one of her classmates saw the elf, then what would she do?

"I . . . uh . . . I didn't mean . . . " she stammered helplessly, then risked a glance at the doorway.

The elf was gone. Arica blinked and rubbed her eyes, feeling relieved and confused at the same time. Maybe he had never been there in the first place. Maybe she had only imagined him. She had been more tired than usual lately — ever since her last trip to Bundelag and that long, gruelling journey to Dragon Island.

"I'm sorry," she said to her teacher. "I don't know what came over me."

As she slunk meekly back to her desk, she hoped she wasn't coming down with a fever, or some strange sickness that might make her see things that weren't really there. There were so many odd illnesses going around these days. But she didn't feel sick, only a little dizzy and confused. After a few minutes of staring at the numbers on the page, she managed to focus her thoughts on her test again. By lunchtime, she almost believed that she had made the whole thing up.

Then after school the elf turned up again. Arica was rounding the corner of the building to join her friends for a quick game of soccer when she bumped into her cousin, Connor, coming from the other direction.

"Oh, there you are!" he cried. "I've been looking all over for you. You'll never believe what's happening! Do you remember the elf, Nue? Of course you do! Well, somehow he's turned up here, and he's joined our soccer game — uninvited. He keeps stealing the ball. Thank goodness he's covered up his pointed ears. But sooner or later someone's going to knock his hat off and find out he's not human." He shivered, imagining the worst.

"Not if I can help it," said Arica, and she took off running.

Winter had come to Alberta, and with it a cold November wind that whipped her hair about her stinging face and snatched her breath away. Snow had fallen a few days ago and disappeared again, leaving behind a playing field of lumpy, half-frozen soil covered with dead brown grass. Soon the snow would return deeper than ever, so they had to play soccer while they still had the chance.

She arrived at the game just in time to see Nue kick the ball, sending it spinning wildly into the air. Three players dived after it, but somehow Nue got caught in the middle. They all went down in a heap of thrashing limbs while the ball sailed merrily away. Arica paused for a moment and shook her head. The poor elf was nearly as bad at sports as he was at riding Grandmother's stallions.

"Oh, wow," said Connor, thudding to a halt beside her. "It's too bad we can't let him stay and play on the other team. He would destroy their game plan in no time."

"That's just what I was thinking," Arica said with a giggle. "Come on, let's get him out of there."

The goalie had caught the ball and sent it hurtling back toward the centre of the field. Arica and Connor sprinted toward Nue. He ignored them and took off after it. Arica made a grab for his arm, but he just elbowed her out of the way and kept on going. Connor had a better plan. He stuck out his foot and tripped the elf in mid-flight, sending him sprawling onto the grass. A minute later they had him well away from the other kids, pinned up against the chain-link fence that separated the schoolyard from the street beyond.

"What do you think you're doing?" demanded Arica.

A stream of gibberish spilled from Nue's mouth. Arica frowned. Connor shook his head as if to clear his ears. Nue saw their confusion and tried talking louder and faster, which worked about as well as spinning tires on ice.

"Of course," Arica said. "It's beginning to make sense now."

"What makes sense?" asked Connor.

When Raden came to Arica's house to kidnap her mother, he had spoken to them in English — though with an unusual accent. It shouldn't have surprised her that her uncle had learned English, for if what he said was true, he had been to Earth many times.

But Nue had been here only once before, and he had stayed inside Grandmother's house the whole time. Grandmother would be furious that he was here again, unless she was the one who sent him. However, Arica doubted this was the case. There were quicker and easier ways of contacting her than sending a scatterbrained elf. In the past, Grandmother had relied on Arica's bond with the unicorns.

"We've got to take Nue to Grandmother's house right now," she explained. "That's where the magic begins. Without that magic, we're never going to understand him." And she headed off, dragging Nue along by the coat sleeve.

Thankfully, Nue decided to cooperate, and they made good time. On Grandmother's street, they paused at the crosswalk to check for cars, then dashed to the other side. A few moments later, they were at her front door. Arica grabbed the key from its hiding place beneath the potted plant and inserted it into the lock. She pushed the door open, yanked Nue inside by his collar, and had him pinned to the wall before Connor even had the door closed behind them.

"Talk fast, and you had better make it good!" she said through clenched teeth.

"I'm so sorry, brave Arica," Nue gabbled. "I meant no harm. I couldn't help myself. I love games. I went to your home just as the Fairy Queen would have wanted, but you weren't there. I searched until I found the place where you go to learn, but there were human children everywhere, and I could see that you were very busy. I was forced to wait outside for you, and while I was there, some of the human children began playing the most marvellous game. Before I knew it, I was running and chasing and kicking."

"Forget the soccer game," snapped Arica. "Why did you come here in the first place? Did Grandmother send you?"

Nue looked frightened, either because of her impatient tone or from something else, Arica couldn't tell. "Not exactly, brave Arica. Not precisely. But when I overheard your grandmother, the Fairy Queen, talking and saw her eyes grow large and her face turn as white as snow, I knew that she needed you in Bundelag, and I thought I could help. I borrowed one of her grey stallions and rode fast and hard. I didn't fail in my duty. Oh, no! I would never let her down!"

Getting useful information out of Nue was like pulling nails out of boards with your bare hands.

"What did you hear the Fairy Queen say?" Arica asked, resisting the urge to shake him till his teeth rattled.

"It is very bad — "

"WHAT is very bad?"

Nue stared at her gravely with his sad, green eyes. He cleared his throat and wrung his hands and cleared his throat again. His mouth opened. And then Arica heard it.

She'd been half expecting it and wasn't surprised at the tinkling of those tiny bells inside her head, sweet and soft and full of the kind of affection that only Wish could give.

True Arica, came the unicorn's anxious plea. *Come quickly. We need you. The Fairy Queen needs you. Bundelag is in terrible danger.*

Chapter 2

Arica let go of Nue so suddenly that he almost toppled to the floor. Beside her, Connor gasped in dismay. In the ensuing silence, the ticking of Grandmother's clock thundered like drumbeats in her ears.

Ironically, it was Nue who snapped Arica out of her shocked stupor, pushing past her and backing toward the kitchen. "It was the Fairy Queen's spies who brought her the terrible news," he blurted. "Very soon the humans of South Bundelag will invade our country with all the might of their great army, and we will certainly be overcome."

"Connor," Arica began, turning to her cousin. But

Arica felt that familiar out-of-control
plunge through blackness . . .

he was already gone. A moment later he returned, carrying the backpack she always kept at Grandmother's house for emergencies along with the one he had recently stashed away for himself.

There was no more need for words as Arica took the pack and hoisted it onto her shoulders. Then she, Connor, and Nue hurried into the kitchen, joined their hands together, and stepped onto the crack that was the doorway to another world. Arica felt that familiar out-of-control plunge through blackness, followed by the jolt of pain as they landed on the concrete floor. They scrambled to their feet, hurried through the cellar door, and dashed down the long, dark tunnel that led to North Bundelag.

They broke out into a silver wonderland of freshly fallen snow and stood blinking while snowflakes settled at their feet and tiny birds twittered in the treetops above. When their eyes finally adjusted to the brightness, Arica glanced around and decided it must be nearly noontime here, for a lukewarm sun hung high in the sky overhead. Nearby, a grey horse pawed at a snowbank, searching for its lunch. Arica hardly had time to conclude that this must be the stallion Nue had "borrowed" from Grandmother, when the thud of hooves on frozen ground and the crackle of brittle branches filled her ears.

The next moment, the trees in front of them parted, and Arica's grandmother, the Fairy Queen of North Bundelag, burst into view astride her second grey stallion. Arica's dear friend, Wish the unicorn, followed closely behind. Wish's father, Light, the enormous silver unicorn Arica had befriended on her first visit here and the leader of his kind, was the last to appear.

Arica's cry of joy at seeing them all again was choked off when she saw Grandmother's grim face.

Grandmother started by thanking them for coming to Bundelag so quickly. Then she turned to Nue, and her eyebrows lowered ominously.

"You took my stallion and went to Earth without

my permission," she said in a voice that sent shivers down Arica's spine. "I realize you meant well, but that's no excuse. Think of the damage you could have done! If you ever pull a stunt like that again, I'll chain you to your own bedpost. Do you understand?"

Arica felt sorry for Nue as he stood and stared miserably at his shoes, but she was certain he wouldn't make that same mistake again. She had taken the brunt of Grandmother's anger a few times herself, and it wasn't a fun experience.

"I understand," he mumbled into his collar.

That seemed to satisfy Grandmother, for she let the matter drop. "As you know," she continued, speaking now to all of them, "I have a network of spies in South Bundelag. We've known for a long time that they were planning a major assault, but we didn't know how or when. Now we do. Their army is so large that the small bridges spanning the River of Songs would have slowed them down. But the river is frozen now, and they are coming. The information my elves have gathered is that the humans will invade North Bundelag eight days from today at dawn."

The breath rushed out of Arica, as if someone had just kicked her in the stomach with a boot. The long-awaited time had come. Grandmother wasn't talking about skirmishes or small battles any longer, but about a full-scale invasion.

"We know where they plan to cross, and be assured that we'll be ready and waiting," she continued. "And we have more force on our side than they know. Arica, because of their friendship with you, the ogres have made a treaty with us. Yet, although they are brave and loyal to us and to our cause, I fear it still won't be enough. That's why I want you and Connor to take Wish and Light north to troll country and ask the trolls to join us."

Arica looked over to Connor to gauge his reaction, and saw his face whiten with alarm. She couldn't see her own, but she was sure it matched his.

"Why us?" she asked, trying to hide her shiver of apprehension from Grandmother. "Wouldn't the trolls respond better to you?"

Grandmother shook her head. "I have no time to spare, and besides, you've had a lot of experience dealing with them."

Arica opened her mouth to protest that none of that experience had been good, but then Light's gentle, worried voice spoke deep inside her mind.

True One, he said. *For hundreds of years, a prophecy has been told among our kind. It says the True One will come, and in our darkest hour she will save us from destruction.*

Arica swallowed the lump of anxiety that swelled suddenly in her throat. How could she fulfill such a destiny? How would she ever accomplish such a task? She had once told Light that she was small and not very brave. In the face of such grave danger she felt even smaller and more frightened than she had ever felt before. She saw Grandmother's firm but worried face, and Connor's willingness in spite of his fear, and as she looked into Wish's noble, trusting eyes, she knew that she had to try. Her own father, the rightful heir to the throne of North Bundelag, had recently told her that whatever he was meant to do, he believed she would do it for him. All she could do was her best and hope it was enough.

She squared her shoulders with a courage she didn't yet feel, and turned toward Grandmother.

"I won't let you down," she said, as Grandmother's strong arms pulled her close. She would have to remember this moment in the difficult days to come — this feeling of love and safety that only Grandmother could give. Stepping back reluctantly from the embrace, she wished that things weren't happening quite so quickly. She still felt a little breathless and carried away by it all.

"Good luck to you both," Grandmother said. "I'll meet you at the Fairy Village five days from now."

Grandmother gave Connor a hug as well, for although he wasn't her grandson, she had always treated him like part of the family. Then she handed him a leather bag that Arica assumed must contain additional food and clothing for their journey.

Finally, Grandmother gave them their swords. Connor buckled his on, hands trembling with excitement. He had just begun to use his when they'd left Bundelag before, and he had surprised everyone, including himself, with his natural skill. Arica's sword was already an old friend, dear to her for its usefulness in this primitive land and because it was once her father's.

Grandmother signalled, and both of the stallions knelt. She and Nue mounted, and the horses sprang to their feet again, prancing and eager to be gone. Grandmother nodded, and they leaped forward, and with a chorus of whinnies and thudding hooves, they disappeared into the trees. A minute later, horses and riders burst from the forest onto open ground. Arica's last sight was of Grandmother's cloak billowing around her and the stallions' tails as they rippled like long grey banners in the wind. Then they were gone.

Arica stood for a moment longer and stared at the place where they had been. Then she took a deep breath, gathered her courage, and turned to Connor.

"Let's get going," she said.

Chapter 3

The unicorns carried them across country at a pace that would have exhausted an ordinary horse within hours. But the unicorns were lighter and swifter than horses, and had the advantage of their magic, which gave them added strength and endurance. Arica knew from experience, however, that if they were pressed long and hard enough, they would eventually grow tired, for they were still creatures of flesh and blood in spite of their amazing powers.

After several hours of steady riding, the cousins stopped to rest and eat their supper. Grandmother's pouch did indeed contain dried meat and fruit, as well as cheese, biscuits, and plenty of small, sweet carrots. As soon as the hurried but badly needed meal was finished, Connor and Arica climbed back on the unicorns and continued their journey.

"What's the best way to go about this?" Connor asked as they rode. "We have no experience in looking for trolls — only in avoiding them."

Arica nodded in agreement. "I've been thinking about it," she said, "and there are two things we know for sure about trolls. One, they prefer to stay in the mountains, and two, Uncle Raden has some working in his mine."

"Ah," said Connor, "the mine. Where you and the elves and unicorns were held captive and forced to work for him . . . "

"That's the place," she agreed grimly. "I don't know where the leader of the trolls lives, or even if there is such a thing, but the way I see it, the mine is the best place to start asking questions."

"You're forgetting one thing," Connor said helpfully.

"What's that?"

"Didn't you say that Raden lives there? He won't take too kindly to us poking around."

"Maybe he won't be home," was all she had to say. But the words gave her little comfort, and she could see that Connor felt just as uneasy as she did.

Later, as the sun sank below a hazy line of mountains to the west and two moons glittered in a rapidly darkening sky, they paused at the crest of a hill overlooking a valley and a ragged mountain beyond. Memories of previous visits to this place flooded into Arica's mind, most of them unpleasant. Tucked beneath the black, foreboding tower of stone ahead lay the cluster of small buildings where she had once been held against her will. From the windows of those small buildings the pale lamplight gleamed.

Was it her uncle? Once he knew they were here, he'd do everything he could to hinder them. Still, they had to take the risk.

We must, urged Light.

For Bundelag, Wish added.

"Are you ready for this?" Arica asked Connor.

"What if I told you no?" he said, but she wasn't fooled. The eyes that met hers were as clear and determined as she had ever seen them.

"That's not the answer I'm looking for," she said, then grinned. He grinned back, his teeth flashing white in the moonlight. Arica knew and understood him well. The more nervous he became, the more he liked to joke around. In the past, this had proved to be a good thing, for his lightheartedness balanced out her serious nature, and often his mind remained clear while hers was clouded with emotion.

Deciding there was no point in waiting any longer, she pushed Wish forward into a gallop, and with Connor and Light at their heels, they plunged downward toward Raden and his mine.

Just as she and Connor had feared, her uncle was home. Worse yet, somehow he had known they were coming and was waiting in the doorway of the first building they approached. He had his ways of tracking people, especially those he didn't trust. She and Connor had probably passed a dozen of his trolls on their way here without even knowing it. There was no creature as sneaky and skilful at spying as a troll, as long as it stayed downwind. She had often wondered how anyone as finicky as Raden managed to put up with the stench of trolls, never mind their crudeness and overall lack of manners.

"My dear Arica," he crooned, when they thudded to a halt in front of him. "What a pleasant surprise!"

She hated the mockery in his voice even more than the sneer on his lips. They were thin, bitter lips, set beneath dark brows, black hair, and a deceptively handsome face.

"Drop it, Uncle," she said. "You knew we were coming. You probably know why we're here. Take us to the troll leader, or tell us where we can find him, or her. Then we'll leave."

"Troll leader?" he said. His eyebrows shot upward, feigning surprise. "What do you need him for, my dear?" he wagged one long finger at her. "Trolls are such distasteful and untrustworthy creatures.

Perhaps I can help you instead."

"Our business has nothing to do with you," she snapped. "So don't try to stop us."

Connor fidgeted beside her and jerked his head. She followed his direction and saw, half-hidden behind a storage building, a wagon piled high and covered with a tarp. It might be nothing, of course. But knowing Raden, that wasn't likely.

"I would never try to stop you," her uncle sneered. "I have more important things to do."

Like gathering supplies and ammunition for the South? she wondered. She stared down at her uncle, too weary to continue this useless conversation. "I can see that now is not a good time," she said. "We'll come back in the morning."

He had known they were coming and was waiting in the doorway . . .

The harsh staccato of Raden's laughter remained in her head long after they had left him far behind.

That night, beneath a broken roof, while the cold, glittering stars of Bundelag peeked through, Arica saw his pale, skull-like face still leering at her from the shadows. And as she tossed and turned on an old bunk abandoned by elves, she dreamed of black eyes filled with hate, and of long, bony fingers reaching for her throat.

They returned to Raden's house at the break of dawn and pounded on his door.

It was a cold, grey morning, with a wind that spit half-frozen rain down upon their heads and groped at them with icy, persistent fingers. It didn't take them long to discover that the coats they had brought from

Earth — fine for the dry, cold weather there — were sorely inadequate for this. Once again, Grandmother had everything under control. While digging around in the bag she had given them, Connor discovered two cloaks of a thin, strong material Arica had never seen. Once on, they were amazingly warm and repelled the moisture completely. She should have known Grandmother would think of everything. On Arica's first few trips to Bundelag it had been summertime and, later, a warm and pleasant autumn. She hadn't expected the cold weather to strike so fiercely.

They knocked on Raden's door repeatedly, and waited in vain for him to answer their summons. After trying the doors of several other buildings, they concluded that he had disappeared, leaving them to fend for themselves. The loaded wagon they had seen the day before was also missing.

It's just as well, True Arica, said Wish. *The fairy Raden didn't intend to give us any information.*

"You're right, of course," she said. "This is all my fault. If I hadn't been so tired and discouraged last night, I might have been able to wring something useful out of him. But now he's gone and it's too late."

But it's not too late to keep looking, said Light. *There are trolls in the mountains north of here. It shouldn't be hard to find them.*

"And there's an elf village as well," Arica added, her heart lifting. "Maybe they know something."

The elves in that village had helped them once before, she remembered, when they had attacked Raden's mine and freed the elves and unicorns that he had imprisoned there.

"What's up?" asked Connor, who'd been waiting patiently throughout a conversation he could only hear one side of. For, although he and Arica were both half-fairy, only she had the ability to speak with the unicorns.

"Get on Light's back again," she said. "We're going to find some trolls."

But Connor never got the chance. The next moment, a troll stepped out from behind a nearby building, followed by another and another. They moved quickly, in spite of the thick arms that dangled to their knees, and their wide, flat feet. Before she and Connor even had the chance to step toward their unicorns, they were surrounded by a dozen smelly, red-eyed trolls, all with their weapons drawn and pointed. Arica stood for a moment in silence and stared at the swords that enclosed them like a ring of ugly, vicious teeth.

"Never mind," she said to Connor. "It looks like they found us."

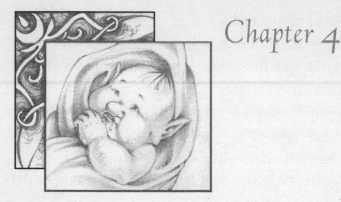

Chapter 4

The trolls seemed to be waiting for them to make the first move.

Arica felt confident that she and Connor could defeat them if it came to an out-and-out battle. Her swordsmanship had steadily improved with time and practice, and although Connor had had less practice than Arica, he had a natural ability she lacked. They had the magic of the unicorns in their favour as well, a fact their enemies understood and clearly respected.

In the meantime, the unicorns had become agitated and were snorting and prancing about, clearly not liking what they saw. Arica noticed the halo of blue around Wish's ears, and wondered if the trolls recognized this as the early warning that it was. Obviously they did, for some of them were casting furtive glances at the beast.

Arica drew her sword while the trolls were still distracted. Connor needed no urging to do the same. By this time, even the block-headed trolls had figured out that, for them, it was a no-win situation. If Raden had put them up to this, they were clearly having second thoughts about it now.

The impasse ended suddenly when another troll strode up and elbowed his way into the centre of the circle. The newcomer paused and glared at his fellows for a long moment, as if sizing up the situation, then shouted out a string of words that made Arica wince in embarrassment. The circle of trolls scattered, leaving her, Connor, and the unicorns alone with their rescuer.

Arica knew him the instant he turned and she got a good look at his face. This beak-nosed, black-toothed individual was Od, one of two trolls who had kidnapped her from Grandmother's cellar and taken her to Bundelag six months ago. Had it really been such a short time? It seemed to her now that she had always been here, that she had been fighting her uncle and his trolls for as long as she could remember.

Od hadn't changed much. He still had the same

hairy arms, surly smile, and thick hulking body he had always had. But the tattered rags of a common troll had replaced the white shirt and blue satin breeches he used to wear, and his pale, warty face looked worn and drawn. Arica wasn't surprised — his time spent as Raden's right-hand troll couldn't have been all that pleasant.

"I've come to make you a deal," Od growled.

Arica gazed around. The other trolls had stopped about twenty metres away and were watching, still ready with their weapons. She wasn't afraid to take the trolls on. But her father always told her that it was better to strike a bargain than to battle, and the latter should only be done as a last resort. In this case, it looked like Od was giving them a way out.

"I'm listening," she said.

"We each have something the other wants," he continued in his bitter, grinding voice. "I received word last night that my child is dying. Your unicorns can heal her. I happen to know that you're looking for the leader of my people. I can take you to him."

Arica could hardly believe their good fortune. This could save them days of searching — provided that Od wasn't lying, of course. He had betrayed her into Raden's hands once before, and this could very well be a trick to slow them down, or even stop them altogether.

"Why should we trust you?" demanded Connor, echoing Arica's own thoughts.

Od snarled a reply. "Because you have no choice."

"That's where you're wrong," Arica snapped back. "There are always other choices. Some are just better than others."

True One, said Light, stepping close to her. *This troll is telling the truth.*

If anyone knew, it would be a unicorn, for they were creatures of pure truth themselves. "All right," she relented. "We'll take a chance. But Od, I promise you that if you betray us, you'll have the Fairy Queen and all her elves to deal with."

Od glared back at her with his dull red eyes. "Do you think I don't know that?" he growled. Then he turned and stomped away.

She and Connor waited with impatience, wondering if he was coming back or if they were meant to follow him. But he returned shortly, leading a horse that was saddled and loaded with supplies. With some reluctance, though they were committed now, they mounted the unicorns and followed Od away from Raden's mine and west into the mountains.

They travelled for most of the day, on a road that was little more than a twisting footpath winding among the shrubs and boulders. Od's thin, scraggy horse was stronger than it looked and clearly not bothered by the rocky, up-and-down terrain and the worsening weather. Arica shuddered to think of where they'd be without Grandmother's cloaks, for an icy wind whistled up the valley, flinging soggy snow into their eyes and ears, and whipping their animals' manes back into their faces.

It was well into the afternoon by the time they neared the base of the final mountain, the only thing left between them and the rock-strewn seashore and the grey, churning ocean beyond. Every muscle in Arica's body ached with fatigue, and all she could think about were hot bubble baths, back rubs, and warm beds.

Od led them through a tangle of shrubs and along a narrow ledge that wound sharply upward to an opening in the rock face above. The cave mouth was large enough to admit all of them at once, including the horse and unicorns, and provided instant relief from the wind and driving snow.

Once they were inside, Od dug into his saddlebag and pulled out a wooden torch that immediately began glowing with a smokeless, heatless flame. An odd tingle passed over Arica's skin, and she knew she was in the presence of magic. Trolls were pasty-skinned and blinked in the sunlight, and she had wondered if they lived in total darkness in their caves. Now she realized that, like every other creature here in Bundelag, they had their own unique powers. When it came to trolls, she admitted she had a lot to learn.

They followed Od down a tunnel that twisted and turned and branched off so many times that Arica became hopelessly confused. Offshoots from the tunnel revealed caverns of various sizes and shapes, many of them teeming with trolls. The smell was so overpowering it made her eyes sting. Did the trolls have nowhere to put their garbage? Then they passed another cavern, and she had her answer. They just piled it wherever they found an empty room.

Naturally the unicorns were suffering more than anyone. Their sense of smell was more acute than any human's, but that wasn't the biggest reason for their discomfort. Unicorns rarely, if ever, ventured this far underground, and the memories Light and Wish had of working inside Raden's mine were still raw and painful in their minds. Light had been bound in chains that drained his magic and prevented his escape. Wish, who was only a foal at the time, had seen her mother suffer in the same way. Unicorns were creatures of air and sunlight, meant for freedom and wide-open spaces. Difficult as coming here was for Arica, she knew it was ten times harder for them.

Connor was loving every minute of it.

"Oh, wow," was all he could say as he peered up and down the corridors and into every room they passed. "Have you ever seen anything like this?"

She hadn't, and she hoped she never would again, but she didn't say so to him.

At last, they paused at yet another cavern — a smaller one than most they had seen. Leaving the animals waiting at the doorway, she and Connor followed Od inside.

The room was nearly bare except for a crude wooden table littered with half-eaten food. A pile of rags lay in one corner and a mound of dirty straw in the other. A female troll was curled up in the straw, her arm over her face and a small bundle pressed against her side. She scrambled to her feet when she heard them, and let loose the most heart-wrenching cry Arica had ever heard. Her pale face puckered. Tears spilled down her cheeks and dripped off her chin. Od clumped across the floor, clutched her in his arms, and held her in a silent, strangely tender way.

Arica turned her face away, too embarrassed to watch, surprised to the point of shock. Her first elfin friends, Perye and Drusa, had once told her that trolls were loyal to no one — not even to their own friends and family. But maybe the elves had been wrong. Od was either very good at acting, or he sincerely loved this female. And if trolls were truly capable of loving, then convincing them to join in defending their country might not be as impossible as she had thought.

When Arica mustered up the nerve to look again, Od had let go of his wife, retrieved the bundle of rags from the straw, and was on his way back to them again. It wasn't hard to figure out what he was holding.

In all her life Arica had never seen anything so ugly and yet at the same time so helpless and appealing. The baby looked like a tiny wrinkled doll with a lump of putty for a nose, two slits for eyes, and a half-open mouth that dribbled something white and wet onto the front of Od's shirt. Each breath the infant took sounded like her last, and her cheeks were crimson with fever. Od hadn't lied about this, at least. The child was obviously very ill.

Od stood and waited impatiently for Arica to make good her part of the bargain. She couldn't help but wonder if he would do the same for her when the time came. Sighing, she took the baby and turned back toward Wish.

When the mother troll saw Arica leaving with her child, she whimpered and tried to come after them, but Od held her back with his hand. Arica understood her alarm. She had probably never seen a unicorn before, and, as Arica well knew, her horned friends had terrified many in this land.

"Wish," Arica said, pausing in front of her and holding up the baby. And as always, Wish knew exactly what to do. Arica watched, entranced once again, as Wish's horn began to sparkle with tiny blue lights. The unicorn waited for a moment as if focusing her power, then lowered her head and gently touched the tip of her horn to the baby's forehead. The magic tingled against Arica's skin as it washed over the baby in her arms, bathing her in colour. A few moments later the healing was complete, and Wish raised her head.

The infant's eyes flew open. She took a look at Arica, Connor, and Wish all peering down at her, sucked in one great gulp of air, and shrieked as though someone had just pinched her little pug nose. Wish reared in alarm. Arica rocked the baby back and forth and stroked her tiny wrinkled cheek.

"Don't cry, baby," she cooed. "You're going to be all right, now." The infant's skin was no longer red and hot, but pale and clammy. This was very good. Pale and clammy was normal for a troll.

Arica glanced up just in time to see the baby's mother descending upon her, howling and flapping. Before Arica even had a chance to explain, the mother yanked the baby out of her arms and whisked it back to the safety of the straw pile.

"You're welcome," said Connor under his breath.

Arica grinned. "I'm sure she'll be thankful when she's over being terrified out of her wits."

Together she and Connor slipped back out into the tunnel so Od could have some time alone with his family. They didn't have to wait long for him. In less than a minute he reappeared, looking vastly relieved and, she was pleasantly surprised to see, almost grateful. But, emotions quickly under control again, his face stiffened into the bitter, boorish mask she knew so well.

"You kept your part of the bargain," he growled. "Now I'll keep mine."

Chapter 5

Od led them back the way they had just come, though it was hard to be sure in such a dark tangle of passageways and rooms. After a stretch of steady climbing, they broke out into the largest cavern Arica had yet seen. A pool of black, fetid water lay to their left. On their right a pathway wound through a clump of glittering stalagmites, ending at the foot of a huge wooden throne.

Arica heaved a sigh of relief. Up until that moment, she hadn't been entirely sure Od wasn't leading them into a dungeon somewhere. Immediately, the sigh turned into a choking cough, for upon the throne sat an enormous troll. No, upon the

throne sat the fattest troll Arica had ever seen. His
cheeks ballooned. His eyes bulged. Fingers like
plump, furry caterpillars rested at his sides. Folds of
jelly-like flesh spilled from beneath his shirt and
down over his belt. Two swollen feet rested on a
stool in front of him. Flame-red, half-mad eyes
under thickset brows blazed at her and Connor as
they followed Od closer to the throne. Something or
someone standing in the shadows behind the troll
king muttered and moved, then quieted again.
Perhaps the king's guard didn't like what he was seeing. Neither did Arica.

Od knelt before the king. Arica choked back her
distaste and forced herself to show the same respect.
Connor fell to his knees beside her, almost eagerly,
beaming like an idiot. "Look at that king!" he
exclaimed. "Don't you think he's impressive?"

"What do you want?" the mound of troll-flesh
bellowed. Then he saw the unicorns, and his pasty-
pale face broke into a sick, delighted leer. Arica
wasn't surprised that the grimace revealed purple,
swollen gums and stubs for teeth.

"Bring them closer!" he boomed. "How did you
capture such a prize? You'll be richly rewarded!" As
he spoke, the spittle sprayed. Arica suppressed the
urge to wipe her sleeve across her face.

"Honourable king," said Od quickly, "these two
fairies were sent here by the Fairy Queen of North

Bundelag. The unicorns belong to them. They have something to ask you."

The king blinked and gawked, as if this was just a bit more information than his feeble brain could process. He stared at them, then at Wish and Light, then back to them again. At last he gathered his wits and spoke.

"What is it?" he bellowed.

"Honourable king," said Arica, giving him the same title that Od had. "Our situation is grim. In seven days the humans of South Bundelag will invade the North. We have little hope of winning without the help of your people. The outcome of this war will affect you as much as it does us. Please give us some of your strongest men. If you do, the Fairy Queen will be forever grateful."

The troll king stared at Arica. She could almost hear the gears grinding as his mind processed the information. Then his eyes widened and a harsh rattle burst from his throat. The disgusting lout was nearly rolling off his throne with mirth! How could he treat them this way when they had come so far? She was icy cold and shivering. Her knees hurt and her head ached, and this was getting them nowhere.

On and on it went, and the louder he laughed, the hotter the anger boiled up inside of her. Remembering that trolls considered manners a sign of weakness, she reached down and drew her sword from her belt.

"Do as I ask," she said through clenched teeth, "or I'll shave the hair from your fat, ugly neck with this and wipe it on your feet."

The king's laughter gurgled to a halt. His goggle eyes bulged and his chin wagged. Connor gasped. Od moaned in fear. Then the figure behind the throne leaped forward, babbled what sounded like a curse, and pointed. An explosion of yellow light burst from the creature's fingertips and hurtled across the cavern, expanding as it came. An instant later, Arica, Connor, and Od were surrounded by a huge, pulsing bubble of raw power.

Arica blinked, realizing too late that here was no ordinary royal guard. Standing before them now was a troll she had met and battled with before — Ega the Enchantress.

But Ega had made a serious mistake. Though the bubble kept them inside and others out, Arica could still feel the minds of the unicorns. That meant she still had access to their magic.

The bubble held very little air, and Od was sucking oxygen like a bellows, howling and flinging himself against the walls of their prison. Connor, gasping for breath but as cool-headed as ever, was hacking at the bubble with his sword, but to no effect. Knowing she had very little time, Arica drew

"Do as I ask," she said through clenched teeth, "or I'll shave the hair
from your fat, ugly neck with this and wipe it on your feet."

power from the unicorns and formed it into a tiny blue ball, small and smooth and hard within her hand. She felt the power as it tingled up her arm and into her veins, warming her insides and wiping away the soreness and the pain. Then she raised her hand and flung the ball directly at the wall of yellow light.

Ega's bubble shattered with a force that flung the three of them face down onto the ground. The unicorns and Od's horse were caught in the blast and staggered back, whinnying with alarm. Ega, who had been standing in front of the throne and the king, was thrown backward into his lap. The king's cup and sceptre, balanced so carefully on the armrest of his throne, bounced and clattered across the floor.

But that was only the beginning. The blue ball continued what it had so efficiently begun. It hit the ceiling, jarring a clump of stalactites, then hurtled down to smash at the horse's feet. A shower of stalactites followed, pinging like nails on tin. That was the final straw for the poor beast, and he whinnied in terror and plunged toward the door. The ball rose again, smacked against a bare patch on the ceiling, and plummeted into the black pool below. Foul, greasy water sprayed in every direction. The liquid frothed and boiled, spitting blue light. The ball rose again, much smaller and paler now, and whacked against the wall behind the king's head like a ripe melon hitting cement. A shower of dust and rock fragments rained down upon Ega and the king. The ball hung in mid-air for a moment, then burst into a hundred tiny sapphires of light that glittered as they fell.

It was over. Ega rolled off the king's lap and frantically brushed at the grime on his royal robes. Arica leaped to her feet, grabbed her sword from the floor, and twisted back toward the king. She heard the hiss of Connor's breath beside her, and an instant later saw why.

The king's eyes blazed. His chest heaved. His skin was mottled red with rage. He rose on his swollen feet and teetered, quivering with fury.

"Get out of my throne room!" he shrieked. "And away from my mountain! I despise fairies even more than I detest elves! I won't let my people get involved in your petty little war! Not now — not ever! Leave while you still can!"

Sick at heart, Arica turned and strode toward the door, dragging Connor with her.

"Wait a minute!" he protested, but she ignored his cry and kept moving. "Are you going to give up so soon?" Connor squawked and wriggled as she pulled him down the tunnel with the unicorns trotting behind them.

"Yes I am," she said flatly. "I prefer my head

attached to my shoulders." Realizing she had no idea where they were or in what direction they were headed, she skidded to a stop and peered up and down the dimly lit passageway.

We know the way, True One, said Light, as he and Wish stepped past her. *Follow us.*

Connor hadn't finished with her yet.

"Running away from a tight spot isn't like you," he reminded her, as they scrambled after the unicorns.

"If you can do better, then go ahead and try," she retorted.

That silenced him for a moment, long enough for Arica to get her thoughts together. What he had said was true, of course. She rarely backed down from a challenge. But as she battled Ega and the king inside the cavern and saw the hatred smouldering in their eyes, she had suddenly realized she couldn't possibly change a thousand years of tradition in a single moment. The trolls despised the elves and fairies because that was what they had always done. That was all they knew how to do.

"Look," she explained at last, "trying to talk them into anything is a waste of time. We could have made the king do as we asked by brute force, but that wouldn't give Grandmother the loyal, committed soldiers she needs. I feel as bad as you do," she added, as Connor opened his mouth to protest further, "but we just don't have time to discuss it — not when I've thought of something better."

"What?" asked Connor, dropping the subject of trolls.

"Dragons," she said.

Chapter 6

That night they camped on a small stretch of sand beside the open sea. Connor found a pile of rocks that gave them some protection from the weather, though, thankfully, the snow was all but gone and the wind had weakened to a stiff breeze. Above them, two moons peeked through rags of racing clouds, and the few stars brave enough to put in an appearance glittered in the sky like hard, bright gems. Nearby, waves boomed out their dance of death, spraying salty tears into the night.

Connor tried to build a fire out of sticks of driftwood, but gave up after the wind doused his tiny flame for the third time.

"Well, it was a nice thought," Arica said, as they sat together in the dark and shivered. She could hear his teeth crunching on biscuits gone dry and stale.

"How will we get to Dragon Island?" Connor asked. "I assume you've worked out the details."

"It won't be easy," she confessed. "We need a ship. And we have to get back to the Fairy Village in time to meet up with Grandmother." She sighed. "The only thing I can think of is to search out the nearest elf village and ask for help."

A short while later, exhaustion overtook them. Wish and Light had been pacing restlessly, but now they could hardly keep their eyes open, so they all curled up together on a bed of sand sheltered by the rocks. Arica's last thought was that one of them should stay awake to stand guard over the others. Then the thought slipped quietly away, as she slid into the blissful oblivion of sleep.

Arica woke with a jolt many hours later, a whisper of warning sounding in her brain.

Wake up, True Arica, said Wish, stirring restlessly beside her. *Someone is coming.*

Arica sat up and peered into the darkness. Nothing moved. Dawn wasn't far off, for the sky above the mountain peaks had paled to charcoal grey, and the moons had travelled almost all the way across the sky. The unicorns' warm breath steamed about her face as she bumped around in the semi-darkness searching for her backpack.

"What is it?" Connor asked sleepily.

"Get up and find your things," she said. "The unicorns have sensed danger, and they're never wrong. We might have to leave in a hurry."

"You're too late!" cackled a familiar voice, and out from behind a boulder drifted a thick shadowy shape, followed by another, and then several more. Words were muttered and torchlight flared, revealing the forbidding, frightful face of Ega the Enchantress.

The glare cast by her wildly flickering torch made her look more ghastly than ever. Harsh light and shadow transformed her face into a gaudy skull set upon a heap of fluttering rags and pallid flesh. Her red eyes glowed and her free hand clawed at the air as she spoke. One of the trolls behind her pushed forward, stamping and snarling. She silenced him with a blow to the head.

"What do you want?" Arica asked warily, preparing to pit magic against magic in yet another fight. Connor moved in closer, fully awake now, and with his sword drawn.

"I paid you a little visit last night, and I couldn't help but overhear something you said," the enchantress sneered. "I've come to make you a deal."

"Why should we bargain with you?" Arica asked,

hardly able to keep her voice civil. "Do you have soldiers to give us? If not, then you have nothing we want."

"Ah, but I think I do," Ega replied in her honey-and-vinegar voice. "I have the fastest ship in North Bundelag anchored just a few kilometres from here. I can get you to Dragon Island in two days — guaranteed."

In the silence that followed, the breaking of waves on rock thundered like cannons in Arica's ears. Did she dare to consider this seemingly generous offer? "What do you want in return?" she asked, steeling herself for a ridiculous answer. Knowing Ega, she would demand precious jewels or gold — something of great value. Could Grandmother afford to pay? Would she want to?

"Nothing — yet," Ega said. She paused and licked her lips, her gaze flickering over to the unicorns and back again. "I need time to think it over. But it will be something well worth my time, I assure you." Her dark eyes, bright and hard as stones, pinned Arica's.

"No deal," Arica said, and turned away, filled with foreboding.

Connor was more willing to talk things over. "You can't expect us to bargain with you when we have no idea what our part of the bargain will be," he pointed out reasonably. "You must have something in mind. Give us a hint, at least."

"I'll put it this way," Ega replied. Her voice had a nasty edge to it. "The girl is the granddaughter of a wealthy queen and a friend to the unicorns. I'm sure there's a way to satisfy me. And the elves can't help you. Their nearest village lies inland. I am your only hope."

"Then we'll fight the war without dragons," Arica insisted.

True Arica, Light urged, *you aren't thinking clearly. What could be more valuable than the freedom of all the creatures in this land? Weigh it carefully in your mind. I think you should accept this offer. It is our only hope.*

"No," said Arica. "I don't trust her."

"I don't trust her, either," said Connor, hearing Arica's part of the conversation. "But at this point I don't see that we have a choice."

Arica shook her head. How could she explain the sick feeling in her stomach or the drum roll of her heart inside her chest?

The boy is right, said Wish. *If you want to go to Dragon Island, then this is the only way. But your fears are justified, True One. The help the troll Ega offers will require something costly in return.*

"What's going on?" Ega whined. "What are they saying? Do you want my ship or not? Hurry up and decide. I warn you, I won't wait much longer!"

Arica sighed and turned reluctantly back to Ega. She could hardly make her lips form the words of her reply. "The unicorns think I should accept your offer," she said.

By noon that day they had arrived at Ega's ship, boarded, and were setting sail for Dragon Island. True to her word, the ship was trim and lightning fast, though filthy as a slop trough and nearly as foul smelling. When the wind failed, Ega's magic filled the sails, driving them across the waves at a remarkable speed, through snow and sleet, dodging icebergs and skirting rocky outcrops. By evening of the next day, the ragged snow-capped peaks of Dragon Island stood still and stark against the far horizon.

The following morning at dawn, Ega's trolls guid-

ed the ship as near to land as they could safely get and dropped anchor.

Take some of my magic, True One, said Light, *and hold it inside of you. Use it to call the dragons. They won't harm you as long as the power isn't turned against them.*

Arica reached up and Light lowered his head. When his horn touched her fingers, she felt the magic tingle through her veins like bubbles of blue fire. The joy of it amazed her every time it happened.

There's a right way to call the dragons, with words spoken in the proper order, Light told her. *Otherwise they will assume you mean harm and attack. The magic

The ragged snow-capped peaks of Dragon Island stood still and stark against the far horizon.

*I have given you will help you to know what to say when the time comes.**

Then Ega's trolls lowered the rowboat into the water, and Connor climbed down over the ship's side. Arica followed, a feeling of unease growing inside her. She looked up at Ega and paused for a moment, then made her decision.

"Get in the boat," she said to the troll. "You're coming with us."

Ega glared, opened her mouth to protest, then thought better of it and climbed down, muttering under her breath. Arica caught Connor's puzzled look and then his sudden flash of understanding. Ega couldn't be trusted — she had proven that time and time again. Of course they couldn't leave her on board with the unicorns. It would be just like her to pull up anchor and sail off, leaving Arica and Connor stranded on Dragon Island.

Then the cousins took up the oars and, with Ega scowling between them, pointed their little boat toward the rocky shore.

Chapter 7

When Arica stepped out onto the stony beach of Dragon Island, a sudden gust of wind curled her cloak about her ankles and whipped her breath away. She stood and stared at the bleak and dismal landscape, not knowing whether to feel relieved that they had actually made it, or terrified that they were here. Only a couple of months ago, she, Connor, and Wish had nearly lost their lives in this place, and now they were back, driven by need and desperation to seek the help of dragons.

Arica stared up at the tower of rock that loomed so majestically above them and tried not to think about what they would shortly have to do. The mountain — dark and fierce and capped with silver snow — looked like an ancient wizard rising from the sea. She shuddered and pulled her cloak more tightly about her shoulders. Never in her worst dreams had she thought she would be back here so soon.

Connor paced back and forth in front of her and squinted at the sky, clearly nervous at the prospect of what lay ahead. Ega had found some mounds of dirt partway up the beach and was poking at one of them with a stick.

Arica's heart fluttered a few times against her ribs. The time had come to call the dragons. What if she didn't get the words right? What if they misinterpreted her and attacked?

"What is it?" asked Connor. "You look even more worried than you did a minute ago."

Before she could answer, they heard an ear-splitting screech from partway down the beach. Arica sprinted toward Ega with Connor on her heels, and it wasn't until they had nearly reached her that Arica realized it had been a cry of satisfaction, not terror. She skidded to a halt, wanting very much to wring Ega's vulture-like neck for the false alarm. Then she saw what all the commotion was about, and the urge grew stronger — but for a different reason.

Ega had speared a pfiper with her stick.

The winged snakes were practically the deadliest predator in all of North Bundelag. They attacked without warning, and their bites contained poison that had a delayed, often fatal, effect. But during Arica's last visit here, she had learned something about them that had changed everything. After saving the life of a large, blue-speckled pfiper, it in turn had saved her, Wish, and Connor from a dragon.

Two things were grossly wrong with what she now saw. One, the pfiper at the end of Ega's spear wasn't an ordinary green one, but a special, blue-speckled one. Two, there wasn't another pfiper in sight.

Arica stared down. The mound at Ega's feet looked like a decapitated anthill. Ega had burned a hole into the frozen ground with magic, and loose dirt lay like spilled blood everywhere. Arica thought for a minute. It was wintertime in Bundelag. She hadn't seen a single pfiper since she got here. The one on Ega's stick had obviously been sleeping beneath the ground and hadn't had a chance.

Arica's brain followed these nasty facts to their logical conclusion.

Beside her Connor did the same. "Bumblebees," he muttered, half to himself.

Arica thought she knew what he was getting at, but she had to be sure. "Tell me," she said.

Connor nodded. "The bumblebees on Earth all die off in the winter except for the queens," he explained. "They crawl into holes and hibernate. In the spring they come out and fly around until they find places to start new colonies. Then they make a nest, build a wax egg cell, and lay eggs in it. The rest, as they say, is history."

"So that old theory of mine about the pfipers having queens and nests might be right?"

Connor looked at the demolished mound. "I'd say so," he replied.

Ega stared blankly at them. "You're both crazy," she said, wiping the dead pfiper off her stick with one quick swipe. Then she tromped over to the next mound and began hacking.

"Stop it!" Arica shouted, lunging forward. She drew her sword and knocked the stick out of Ega's hand, sending it flipping end over end across the ground. Ega screeched in outrage, yellow lights flickering around her fingertips.

Arica forced herself to speak calmly.

"I don't have time for this," she said. "Please, just stay here with Connor and be quiet. I have a job to do."

Arica closed her eyes, emptied her mind of all thought, and commanded the magic inside of her to do its work. She felt the power flow through her and out of her in a great rush of sparkling blue light. And when it was over she had no idea what she had just said, for the words were gone, carried away by the unicorn's magic.

For a time, she and Connor and Ega just stood

there and stared up into the sky.

Then the dragon came. It banked on the wind, its spiked scales winking in the sunlight like shards of smoked glass. Its giant, snakelike face turned in the sky, and two eyes as hot as flares burned down upon them. Wings of black satin stretched over bones beat in the air like drums. The great beast settled closer to the earth, tossing dust and sand into their faces. They stood and trembled, shielding their eyes, until at last the dragon sank, dark and glittering, to the sand.

Arica couldn't tear her eyes away from the enormous beast in front of her. She hadn't thought it was possible for any creature to be more formidable than the red dragon they had encountered on their last visit here. Yet this one was even larger and more terrifying.

Heat shimmered off the ebony plating of its body and wafted from between its great armoured jaws. She felt weak and just a little dizzy, until she realized she had stopped breathing. The air she drew into her lungs was flaming hot and reeked of sulphur.

Arica shook herself, as if casting off the last dark tendrils of some terrible nightmare. She tried to lick her lips, but her tongue was parched and dry.

"Light said the dragon would choose someone to talk to," she whispered.

The great beast's hot yellow eyes burned a path

across them, pausing a moment on Ega and then dismissing her, flaring a little at Arica. At last they settled on Connor and remained there. The dragon had chosen.

Arica had admired her cousin when he figured out that the *Book of Fairies* was not the real one, and insisted they go back for it. She had admired him even more for refusing to remain behind when Raden kidnapped her mother and for helping her discover the secret of the rainbow flowers. But she had never admired him as much as she did at this moment. He glanced at her briefly, then raised his chin and pushed his glasses firmly onto his nose.

"I will do my best," he said, then strode bravely forward.

"Don't look into its eyes!" Arica called out. "You'll get caught in the magic!" Then she remembered that Connor *had* to get caught in the magic, for that was the way he would communicate with the great beast.

Arica trembled for her cousin. She couldn't save him, no one could, for the dragon's magic was already upon him, and the rest of them as well. She could hear it chiming in her own bones and even taste it, dark and bitter, on her tongue. She stumbled forward on limbs too weak to hold her upright and fell flat on the ground, caught at the edge of the creature's awesome, eerie power. Though she was too stunned to move, enough of its magic was reaching her that she understood every word it said.

"What do you want, little boy?"

Its words stabbed like hot pokers through her brain. She could only imagine what they were doing to Connor.

"We've come a long way to ask for your help," Connor explained in a thin, high voice. "North Bundelag is in terrible danger. In four days humans from the South will attack, and our army isn't large or strong enough to hold them off. We've already talked to the trolls. They have refused to join us. Will you come, Black Dragon? We need you."

Anger stabbed hot and hateful from the dragon's heart.

"Troublesome boy," it said, **"you are either very brave or very foolish. I am only one dragon, but if you ask each of us in turn, we will all tell you the same story. We were driven from your land hundreds of years ago. Now this island is our home. Fight your own battles, little one, and leave us to ours. We owe you nothing."**

With a clatter of metallic scales and a thunder of

"What do you want, little boy?"

wingbeats, the dragon rose like a great black bird into the sky. And as the magic hold upon Connor's mind wrenched and tore free, he toppled forward, like a discarded bone spat into the sand.

Chapter 8

Back on the cold deck of Ega's ship, Arica didn't think things could get much worse.

Not only had she failed miserably at the one task Grandmother had asked her to do, but her decision to seek the help of dragons had turned out to be a mistake and had put her in Ega's debt as well. How could she face Grandmother with such a sorry tale?

She leaned against Wish, stroking the unicorn and getting what comfort she could from her friend's warm side. What she feared more than anything was that North Bundelag would lose the war. If that happened, she might never see the unicorns again, and worse yet, magic could disappear from Bundelag forever.

And beneath these fears wormed the worry of her debt to Ega and the dreaded price she would have to pay.

The troll ship sailed swiftly southward, and by early afternoon they could see the east coast of North Bundelag lying dark and hazy against the far horizon. They continued to travel all night and most of the next day, following the coastline as it curved around toward the west. At suppertime Arica recognized the landmarks, and instructed Ega to lower the sails and anchor the ship offshore.

None of them could see the Fairy Village, of course, for it was hidden by a magic spell that allowed only fairies and unicorns to enter. Its location had always been a well-guarded secret, but with war looming, Grandmother was using the area as a gathering place for her army. Arica worried that everyone in the entire country now knew where the Fairy Village was.

Ega took them ashore in her rowboat, while the unicorns swam alongside. She sat with the oars on her knees and smirked as they splashed up onto the beach.

"I'll let you fight your pathetic excuse for a war before I collect what you owe me," she called. "And you'd better not try to cheat me. If you escape into that other place of yours, I'll track you down and kill you, fairy or no fairy!"

The cackle that followed rattled painfully inside Arica's skull long after Ega was gone, and the walk from the beach to the Fairy Village had never seemed so difficult or so far. But then she had never had to wade through thigh-high, ice-crusted snowdrifts to get there, either.

When they crossed the magical border into the Fairy Village, Arica was surprised and delighted to see no sign of winter. Children still darted over lawns and peeked out from behind hedges, their laughter tinkling like music in the air. Springs of water still bubbled from beneath boulders and spilled through gardens bright with flowers. The Fairy Queen's castle soared high above the cottages as it had always done, and sunlight still dazzled from above. But even here, war was pressing down its heavy hand, for she saw few men and much worry and sadness in the women's eyes.

War was never easy for anyone — no matter what world you lived in.

As she and Connor made their way toward the castle, Arica noticed they had attracted a crowd of small followers. Wide, bright eyes stared in fascination at the unicorns. A few of the braver children crept close enough to steal a touch from Wish, who was smaller and less intimidating than her father. Only one boy approached Light, and he was rewarded by being allowed to stroke the magnificent stallion's nose.

Arica couldn't help but smile as he dashed away, whooping with delight, to tell his mother.

As they neared the Fairy Queen's castle, Arica looked across the drawbridge and saw Doron, the Keeper of the Village, walking out to meet them.

It amazed her that he always knew when they were coming. It wasn't like at home, where you could telephone ahead. She

Only one boy approached Light…

had concluded long ago that this unique knowledge was part of the power that he possessed, for every time she met him, she saw magic burning in his eyes.

"True One," Doron said, taking her hand. His fingers seemed as fragile as silk-covered twigs, but his grip was firm and sure. "Connor," he said, turning to the boy. "It's good to see you again." Then he lowered his head as a sign of respect for the unicorns.

"Light and Wish. As always, it's a privilege to have you here."

After the greetings were done, Doron led them up over the drawbridge and into the castle where Arica's grandmother, the Fairy Queen of North Bundelag, sat waiting for them in the Great Hall. When Grandmother saw them, she rose from her chair at the huge oak and ebony table and stepped forward to meet them.

Up to this point, Arica had done quite well at keeping her feelings in check. But when she saw the lines of worry and weariness etched on Grandmother's face and saw them melt away at the relief of seeing her again, Arica could no longer hold back the tide.

"Grandmother!" she blurted out as she rushed into the Fairy Queen's arms. Then she burst into tears.

Arica remained there, safe in the circle of her arms, while Connor filled the Queen in on everything that had happened. He described how they had failed to convince the trolls to join their cause. He told her about their journey to Dragon Island and the price that was hanging over their heads.

When he was done, the Fairy Queen looked long and seriously into Arica's tear-filled eyes. She spoke without a trace of anger or blame. "You dared to try what I had not even considered as a possibility. The result can hardly be called failure."

Arica made a gulping, sobbing sound against Grandmother's shoulder.

"And as for Ega," Grandmother continued, "it is possible that in a few days no one in North Bundelag will be free to do anything, let alone carry out petty personal transactions. If we are successful in fighting off the invasion, I will speak to Ega on your behalf. I am sure something can be worked out."

Arica nodded, her sobs subsiding. Grandmother had forgiven her, and although nothing was solved yet, she no longer felt as if she was carrying the burden all by herself. "Thank you," she murmured, feeling immensely relieved.

"You're welcome," the Fairy Queen said. "Now come with me, and let's find you brave travellers something to eat."

———

Grandmother was up before dawn helping her army prepare for departure, and by midmorning she returned to tell Connor and Arica it was time to go. The cousins stared in amazement at the meadow beyond the Fairy Village — it was packed to overflowing with fairies, elves, and ogres. In some places the snow was knee-deep, while in others it was trampled down to sheets of ice. Campfires crackled, scattering smoke and ashes to the wind. Men of all kinds shouted, jousted, and milled about.

Yet somehow this motley assembly organized itself

into ranks and columns behind its leader, the Fairy Queen of Bundelag, and began to follow her west across the open plain that lay south of the Badlands. The army crossed the frozen Black River, and then, at the same steady pace, made its way southwest through a small forest to the bank of the River of Songs.

Arica had not been sorry to miss the evil whispers of the Black River, but she was disappointed to discover that this river's voice, too, had been stilled by winter's frosty grip. She missed the river calling to her, pulling at her with the pleasure of its song. As they paused beside it, Grandmother informed them that in about thirty-six hours, the human army would cross at this spot and begin their assault.

Grandmother set up camp in a partially wooded area on a hill overlooking the valley of the River of Songs, and went off to inspect her troops. Arica sat alone in the doorway of the tent and tried to eat her supper of cheese and berry cake, but her hunger had abandoned her. On the south side of the river, a thousand enemy fires glowed in the darkness like a host of city lights. By tomorrow night there would be a thousand more. Worry twined its long, insistent fingers about her throat, making it hard for her to swallow, and tied her stomach into painful knots. How could they hope to win against an army twice the size of their own? To make matters worse, they were armed only with swords, spears, and bows and arrows — no match for the humans and their guns.

But we have magic, True Arica, said Wish, emerging from the bushes behind her.

Arica stroked the silken nose that lowered to brush against her cheek. "Shame on you for listening in on my private thoughts," she scolded. "I didn't forget about the magic. I'm just afraid it won't be any match for technology."

What is technology? asked Wish.

"That's a little hard to explain . . . " Arica began.

The bushes suddenly rattled behind them; then came the dull clump of heavy feet. Twigs crackled. Branches creaked. Arica jumped to her feet and grabbed her sword. Wish tensed, every muscle instantly ready to fight or flee. Then something large and dark burst out from behind a tree and blundered to a halt only metres from where they stood.

Arica set her sword down on a rock and reached out her hand to reassure Wish, but the unicorn already knew. A young and rather large ogre girl stood in front of them, her single eye blinking rather stupidly in the light of their tiny fire.

"Thilug!" Arica cried with delight, reaching for the child's fat-fingered, grimy hand. Arica had stopped being bothered by all the dirt in Bundelag a long time ago. This was her friend, a girl she had once saved from choking on a bone. In return,

Thilug's father had given her an ogre eye, and in a battle with the dark unicorn, Shadow, that eye had saved her life.

"Ogres fight
with all their might,
to keep a friend
from a very bad end," Thilug said.

Arica smiled — always speaking in rhyme was one of the many odd but endearing things about ogres. She could see that Thilug had grown since the last time they were together. She was the same height as Arica now, and three times wider. Her thick-limbed body was shaggy with hair, except for the occasional patch of brown, calloused skin. Her nails were like claws, and when she spoke, saliva sprayed from between her crooked, yellow teeth.

Arica adored her.

"You're right, Thilug," she said. "You're helping to keep *all* of us from a bad end. Thank you, and thank your father for me, will you?"

Thilug nodded with enthusiasm and continued:

"Father says
when the war is done,
you should come visit
and have some fun."

As much as Arica cared for these creatures, sleeping on rocks in smelly damp caves and eating half-raw meat wasn't exactly her favourite way to spend a weekend. How could she get out of this without hurting the ogre girl's feelings?

She was saved for the moment by Connor. Returning from his wanderings, he dashed into the clearing, tripped over a rock, and fell flat on his face — still clutching something to his chest. It wasn't until he scrambled to his feet and straightened his glasses that he saw Thilug.

Connor had never seen an ogre this close before. And certainly not on a dark night, with firelight flickering over a square, ugly face that fixed him with a green, one-eyed stare.

Connor took one look, let out a yelp, and jumped backwards. Thilug was even more startled than he was and began to howl at the top of her lungs. There was no use shouting at her, of course. There wasn't a fairy alive with lungs that could match an ogre's. Instead Arica grabbed Thilug by one of her tree-stump arms and yanked, trying to stop the uproar. Wish was prancing about and spitting blue light, a sure sign that she was irritated.

Then suddenly Grandfather popped into existence directly over their heads.

Chapter 9

For Thilug, Grandfather was the final straw. She fled into the bushes, bumping and crashing all the way. Wish, however, had known the fairy elder since she was a foal and was feeling more comfortable now that the howls had subsided. The little blue lights immediately faded from around her horn. As for Connor, he had met the man once or twice before and grinned with delight.

Arica's grandfather, thanks to the evil spell cast by an old enemy, no longer had a solid body. He could travel rapidly from place to place, appearing in mid-air whenever he had an urgent message to deliver. The problem was he couldn't stay visible for long —

and he couldn't get to the point, either. He almost always faded out in mid-sentence, leaving Arica to grind her teeth in frustration.

"Arica," Grandfather began without preamble, "the time has come. Only you can save North Bundelag. Don't ever give up. You're much stronger and braver than you think."

Arica shook her head. She was becoming annoyed. "You told me all this before," she said. "What do you mean only I can save North Bundelag? What exactly am I supposed to do?"

Grandfather stroked his beard thoughtfully with his fingers. "You'll know soon enough," he said, as maddeningly vague as ever. His body was already fading. Arica groaned. The light of two moons beamed right through him to the ground below. Maybe she could squeeze in one more question.

"Grandfather," she said in a rush, "the elves have a prophecy that a fairy with great powers will some-day unite North and South Bundelag. How can that happen when the two countries are such bitter ene-mies?"

The fairy elder was almost gone, but his words drifted back to her like the last notes of a sad, sweet song. "It will happen, my child, but not yet. Only win this battle, and the humans will see the fairies as equals, as a people to be reckoned with, not con-quered and enslaved . . . "

He was gone, leaving Arica and Connor staring at the place where he had been. "I wish he wouldn't do that all the time," she muttered. "It gets tiresome."

Connor grinned at her and proudly held up a book. So that's what he'd been hanging onto so tenaciously. Arica recognized it as the *Book of Fairies*, the ancient collection of fairy writings that contained her people's prophecies and their laws, as well as the names of all the living fairies.

"I brought this from your grandmother's castle, and I've been reading it," he explained. "I think I know what you're supposed to do."

Arica and Connor sat down side by side on a log next to their little fire and opened the book. Then Connor, immensely pleased with himself, pulled a flashlight from the pocket of his cloak and flicked it on.

Arica frowned. "Did you *ask* me if you could borrow that?" she said, mildly annoyed. She was sure hers was the only flashlight in North Bundelag.

"I did," he said. "Earlier this evening. You didn't answer me, though. I think your mind was on other things."

She sighed and watched as he thumbed through the pages. She knew that she needed to get a grip on herself. As the time for the battle grew closer, little irritations were becoming more and more difficult to handle, and every molehill seemed like a mountain.

Connor paused near the middle of the book, at a chapter titled "Prophecies." He continued squinting and flipping until he found what he was looking for.

"Here it is," he said, pointing.

She took the book from his hands and read the prophecy. It was short and simple, but it echoed the words that Light had spoken in her mind the day she came back to Bundelag . . .

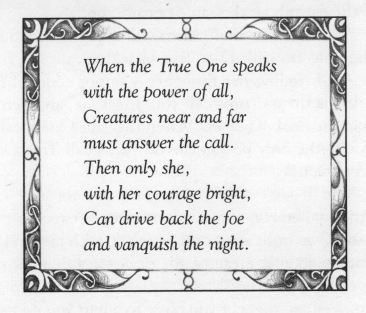

When the True One speaks
with the power of all,
Creatures near and far
must answer the call.
Then only she,
with her courage bright,
Can drive back the foe
and vanquish the night.

Arica groaned. "I'm terrible at solving riddles," she sighed. "This sounds like something Grandfather wrote."

Connor hooted with glee at her small joke. "That's why you brought *me* along!" he said. "I love riddles, and this one wasn't too hard to figure out.

I just had to think about it for a while."

"And?" she asked.

"I got to thinking about prophecies. There's a lot of them around here in Bundelag. There's that elvish one you mentioned to your grandfather, and there's this one, and then there's the unicorns — you told me on the way to troll country what Light had said. And they all seem to be about the same thing. What if they are about the same person, too?"

"You mean . . . me?" Arica wasn't persuaded. Sure, the unicorns called her True One, but . . .

As if reading her thoughts, Connor added, "You told me the unicorns call you True One, and here it is in the *Book of Fairies*: 'When the True One speaks.' You're the only person the unicorns call True One, aren't you?"

"But I don't speak with the power of all," said Arica miserably, reminded again of her recent failures. "The trolls want nothing to do with me, and no one could ever presume to speak for a dragon, not even Grandmother."

"Well, maybe, but you have to admit you do have a unique gift of communication. You talk to unicorns, to elves, to ogres, to your grandfather — "

Arica shook her head stubbornly. "So do you! Except for the unicorns, of course."

"What about the pfipers?" Connor persisted. "They were everyone's enemy, until you came along!"

Connor paused near the middle of the book, at a chapter titled "Prophecies."

Arica scratched her head. "I suppose . . . " she said.

"You called the fairies home, and they came. You asked the rainbow flowers for help, and they answered your plea. Even when you battled Shadow on Mine Mountain, you must have made a silent cry for help, because the magic in the ogre eye responded. Am I right?"

"I don't know." Arica sighed unhappily. "If I have this special talent, why wasn't I successful with the troll king? And the black dragon? I called to it, didn't I?"

"Maybe Ega's nasty magic was interfering both times. I don't know. But you have to admit it's possible."

"Maybe," Arica grudgingly agreed. "But what am I supposed to do now, stand on the battlefield and yell, 'Help! Help!'?"

"Actually, yes!" Connor replied. "Just give it everything you've got — your own talent, the unicorns' magic, and the *Book of Fairies.*"

He paused, and when she didn't speak, he continued. "The rest of the prophecy is easy. It means that with the help of all those that come, you'll stop the humans from conquering North Bundelag."

Did she dare to hope he was right? All he had said made perfect sense. And what did she have to lose? The worst that could happen was they'd end up right back where they started.

"All right," she relented. "Tomorrow is the last day before the battle. Sometime during the morning the rest of the unicorns should arrive from Unicorn Valley. I'll gather them together, and we'll give it a try, though I have no idea how to even begin."

Connor smiled. With his round pale face and his tousled hair and his glasses glinting in the flashlight's yellow glare, he looked like a wide-eyed, feather-headed owl that was very pleased with itself. "I'm sure you'll figure it out," he said, sounding wise and confident.

She wished she felt the same.

Chapter 10

Morning brought with it a cold, dreary wind from the north and a dusting of snowflakes as delicate as down. Arica woke, rolled from between her blankets, and poked her head through the tent flap to find Grandmother standing nearby, peering out across the valley toward the south. Worry and lack of sleep had etched lines like tiny scars across her skin and painted purple shadows underneath her eyes. Arica got up and joined her. Following her Grandmother's gaze, she had no trouble pinpointing the source of concern. A thin but steady line of soldiers was arriving to join the human army, stretching southward as far as the eye could see. Though Arica couldn't make out the details from this distance, she had to assume that many of the soldiers carried guns.

Grandmother knew right away what Arica was thinking, probably because she was thinking the same thing.

"We estimate that nearly a third of the enemy has firearms," she explained, "and I've been pondering the problem for days." She gazed deeply into Arica's eyes. "We're going to need you and the unicorns, dear granddaughter."

Arica nodded, unable to keep the excitement out of her voice.

"I know. Connor and I have a plan that involves the unicorns. There's a prophecy in the *Book of Fairies* that says when the True One calls, help will come."

Grandmother looked thoughtful and gazed out across the valley for a moment. Then she turned back toward Arica.

"It won't hurt to try, of course, but don't get your hopes too high. You know my thoughts on the *Book of Fairies* — some truth, with a lot of wishful thinking. So let's focus on a practical solution. We can use the unicorns' magic as a weapon, in much the same way you once used it to kill pfipers, or you can use it to protect our army from the bullets."

Arica recalled a ground littered with pfiper bodies and shuddered. "I don't want to kill anyone unless I have to," she said.

Grandmother nodded in agreement. "Still, the amount of magic you'll need to protect our army will draw enormous amounts of power. The unicorns will soon become exhausted."

Arica knew that was true. "And when their magic is gone, then what?"

"I'm sure by then we'll have driven the humans back far enough that they'll return to their home-land and leave us alone."

"I hope so," said Arica. It sounded like a workable plan, and she would do everything she could to help Grandmother. But she would still try to make the call beforehand, just as she and Connor had planned.

A thin but steady line of soldiers was arriving to join the human army.

A short time later, as she was gathering wood for the fire, she heard something moving behind her.

True Arica, said Wish, stepping close and blowing warm air on her cheek. *The unicorns will be here soon. Would you like me to call them together?*

Dear, sweet Wish. She was, and always had been, so helpful and generous. But this strength was also her greatest weakness, for in the past it had compelled her to make huge sacrifices that had put her life at risk. Arica stroked the unicorn's nose and pressed her cheek against the silken mane. Newly fallen snowflakes glittered on each strand of hair, strung like tiny diamonds on a thread. Arica blew, and they drifted silently away. The closeness she and Wish shared used to fill her heart with joy. Now all it did was remind her of everything she might lose.

"Yes, Wish," she said, blinking to hold back the tears. "That would be wonderful."

Arica hugged her friend goodbye and headed back to the campsite. She arrived just in time to see the tent flap fly open and a tangle of arms and legs and blankets tumble out. The tangle became a boy who sat up, rubbed his eyes, then pulled his glasses — miraculously unbroken — out of his pocket, and propped them on the bridge of his nose. His hair resembled a porcupine scared half out of its wits, and his clothes looked like they'd spent the last week in a knot under his bed. But, as was usual for Connor in the morning, he was rested, in good spirits, and eager for action.

"What's for breakfast?" he cried, jumping to his feet.

Grandmother looked up when he spoke, and smiled. "Whatever you can find for us," she said, "and thank you for offering." Connor just grinned back at her, not the least bit offended, and started digging through the bags.

After they had breakfasted on biscuits, cheese, raisins, and apples (no sweetened cereal or fancy pastries here), Grandmother took them on her rounds. As they visited the troops of fairies, ogres, and elves in their bustling camps nearby, Arica was amazed, pleased, and relieved to see how many had rallied to join their cause. Spirits were high, and the love they all had for their country and their freedom glowed in their eyes and soared in their voices. Their excitement, she knew, wasn't in anticipation of the fighting, but in the belief that they could win. Tents had been pitched, bedrolls readied, fires started, and food set out. Swords and spears were being sharpened in preparation for the coming battle.

As they marched into an elf camp, Arica surprised herself by laughing out loud. She had never seen so many big green eyes and pointed ears in one place. It was the first glimmer of happiness she'd felt in days. Suddenly two arms were flung around her neck, and another much stronger one gripped her waist, crushing ribs and squeezing out air. A kiss landed on her cheek (Drusa). A hand thumped her between the shoulder blades (definitely Perye). Fingers became tangled in her hair. An elbow jabbed her stomach at the same time as booted feet trampled on her toes. Finally she couldn't take it any more and pushed them away, laughing with the sheer joy of it all. Then Connor caught up with them and the whole performance started all over again.

When the excitement finally died down, Perye and Drusa begged them to stay for lunch, but a shake of Grandmother's head told them there was no time. With a pang of regret, Arica left her friends behind, and by noon they were back at their own camp to find Wish and a clearing full of unicorns waiting patiently for their return.

Arica had never seen such a breathtaking sight in her whole life. Not since the beginning of her travels to Bundelag had the unicorns all come together like this, for even at home in Unicorn Valley they wandered freely.

Including the colts and fillies, she estimated at least a hundred animals. They filled the clearing and spilled over into the forest, their bodies gleaming among the dark, leafless branches of the trees, like lilies caught in thorns. She glimpsed Light and Song, Wish's mother, and recognized a few others she had encountered before. Her magic could tell her each unicorn's name if she concentrated for a moment, but right now she had more pressing things to do. Still, each time her gaze rested on a unicorn, she felt as if she'd known it all her life.

A sudden urge swept through her, so overwhelming that it made her ache all over. If only she could walk among them for a time. If only she could touch them and talk to them and feel the soft, sweet music of their magic in her bones.

But that wasn't why they had come. They had come so she could strip their power from them and use it as a weapon in the war against the humans. The fact that it would protect them and everyone else didn't make her feel any better about what she had to do. Unicorns were never meant for war.

"Oh, wow," said Connor.

"I know what you mean," she agreed. "I've never seen anything so beautiful."

The unicorns waited, a hundred pairs of eyes fixed trustingly upon her. She realized that now was as good a time as any to make the call for help — if she could just figure out how. She paused, considered what to do next, and knew almost immediately. Taking the *Book of Fairies* from Connor's outstretched hands, she opened it to the prophecy and gazed at it for one long moment. Fairy magic tingled in her fingertips and shivered over her skin until she could not longer deny that these four hundred-year-old words had been written about her and for her and because of her — it was only her fear and doubt that had kept her from believing. Grandfather had been right all along, and finally, at last, she knew exactly what to do.

She pulled magic from the unicorns until it boiled in her veins and sang like flutes and trumpets in her bones. The buildup of power was enormous, far greater than anything she had ever experienced before. The skin on her arms and hands glowed blue, and she felt the hair on her head rise up as if lifted by a sudden gust of wind. Connor stared at her and at the spitting, sparkling haloes that now surrounded the unicorns, and his cheeks reddened with excitement.

"This is the coolest thing I've ever seen!" he said.

She wanted to tell him that it felt even cooler than it looked and that she wished he could experience it with her, but the magic didn't allow her time for words.

Her mind expanded higher and wider until it seemed to soar across the land from the north to the south and from the east to the west. She saw the pfipers sleeping beneath the soft white blanket that winter had laid upon them. She saw sparrows huddled in treetops and rabbits curled inside their burrows. Wolves prowled through forests of spruce and pine and howled beneath a pale northern sun. Trolls worked and fought and feasted inside their mountain caves, and dragons soared over waves as tall as clifftops, while sunlight shimmered on their thin, translucent wings.

Then Arica reached out with all the might of the magic she possessed to every creature in North Bundelag, from one far corner to the other. "Come," she said to each and every one. "Come and help us. We need you. We need you."

She stopped. Something was terribly wrong. She felt it deep in her bones, even as her plea for help was done. The unicorns' power twisted and shrank inside of her an instant before it finished what it was meant to do, collapsing in upon itself like a house of straws.

Then it was over, and she fell face first into the snow and knew no more.

Chapter 11

"What went wrong?" Connor asked.

They were huddled beside a fire that Connor had rekindled from the ashes of the old one, but even with the flames flickering on one side of her and Wish pressed up against the other, Arica couldn't quit shivering. The *Book of Fairies* lay open on her cousin's lap.

"When the True One speaks with the power of all — " he puzzled for the fifteenth time, "Creatures near and — "

"Oh, no," Arica moaned with sudden understanding and buried her face in her hands.

"What?" he asked, glancing up in alarm.

"The power of ALL," she said as her hands dropped back into her lap. "The power of all the *unicorns*. Don't you get it?"

Connor only had to think about it for a moment. "Shadow," he whispered, sending her a look that was only slightly less stricken than the one she was giving him. "We forgot about Shadow."

"When the prophecy said all of the unicorns, that's exactly what it meant," she said, wondering how she could have been so stupid. "Not all of them, except for one."

She gazed up at the sun still cresting in the sky, then over at the unicorns. Some of them had drifted away in search of food and water, but Arica knew they would return when she needed them. The snow had stopped falling for the moment, but the icy wind that gusted through the trees seemed bent on making their lives as miserable as possible. She struggled to her feet, still weak from her failed spell, and retrieved her backpack and sword from beneath a nearby tree.

"Where are you going?" demanded Connor.

"Where do you think?" she said.

"If you're going to look for Shadow, then I'm coming with you!" he exclaimed. He leaped to his feet and started digging around for his belongings that were buried somewhere in the snow. Arica had often wondered how such an intelligent boy could be so disorganized. He couldn't even keep track of things in his own bedroom, and that was a confined space.

"No. I have to go alone."

He frowned and opened his mouth to protest, then closed it again when logic took hold. Months ago, Connor had journeyed to South Bundelag with them to retrieve the *Book of Fairies*, and he knew how things were between her and Shadow. He knew that only Arica could win the unicorn's trust, and that it would best be done on her own.

It was extremely unlikely that Shadow would agree to help them. The situation was a tricky one and fraught with complicated issues — the main one being Shadow's hatred of the other unicorns. Several years ago, Shadow had accidentally found his way to Earth and, with his horn no longer visible, was mistaken for a horse and badly mistreated. When he returned to Bundelag, the other unicorns couldn't tolerate his wildness and drove him out of Unicorn Valley. The bitterness had been festering inside of him ever since. "How will you find him?" Connor asked.

It was a good question and one of the few problems they faced that had an easy answer.

"I'll ask the unicorns," she said. "If he's anywhere near, they'll know."

I'll help you, True Arica, offered Wish.

Connor still looked unhappy at being left behind.

"Goodbye, then," he said, as she mounted Wish and headed into the forest. He waved as she rode away, looking small and forlorn beneath the trees that rose tall and dark around him. "Good luck!" was the last thing she heard him say.

An hour later, Arica still hadn't found Shadow, though she and Wish had sensed the dark simmering of his magic nearby and were following it. In the process of searching, she came across a small encampment in a clearing. She noticed the tent first. Beyond it she saw a fallen tree and a man sitting on it, roasting a chunk of meat over a fire.

The man was her Uncle Raden.

When he saw her, he rose from the log. She stopped some distance away and waited without dismounting.

He wore a heavy black robe and leather boots to protect him from the cold. Wind gusted about him, sending locks of hair slithering over his face like thin, dark snakes. A couple of his trolls rose from a snowbank behind him and shuffled forward, grunting and grumbling their displeasure at the disturbance, or at the cold, or even the lack of good food. Knowing trolls, it was probably all of those reasons and more.

"What are you doing here?" Arica said. "I don't imagine you brought them to join Grandmother's army." Surprised at seeing him here — the last place

Wind gusted about him, sending locks of hair slithering over his face like thin, dark snakes.

she expected — and impatient to return to her search for Shadow, she forgot to be cautious.

He studied her without emotion. Here in the clear winter sunlight, his eyes were grey and calm, but this wasn't how she remembered them. She had watched his anger turn them black with rage more times than she cared to think about, and she knew she shouldn't let her guard down in his presence. She sat up straighter on Wish's back, her hand hovering over her sword.

"My dear niece," he said, in a voice laced with mockery and spite. "What a pleasure. And how right you are."

"What are you doing here, then?" she asked, expecting only a taunt for a reply. But she had misjudged his intent. He was more in the mood for boasting.

"To watch my southern human friends remove the crown from my mother's head and place it on my own," he said.

Arica had always known he was a traitor, but this was altogether too brazen, even for him. Banishing him to South Bundelag for a time might have been Grandmother's worst mistake. If what he was saying was true, then he'd made friends in some very high places.

"What did you promise to give them in return for this great honour?" she asked.

"Money," he said. His eyes rested for an instant on Wish. "And magic."

"I have no time for this," she said, choking down anger. "I'm looking for Shadow."

"Shadow?" Raden sneered. "I defy you to get anything useful out of that one. He's as miserable and uncooperative as ever. Not that any of that matters. He'll soon be in my power, as well as the rest of his despicable kind."

Arica didn't bother to answer. She had learned something interesting — her uncle and Shadow weren't as chummy as they used to be. The knowledge gave her hope. But as she and Wish galloped away from the clearing, Raden's laughter echoed harshly behind them. The thought of him on the throne of North Bundelag sent a cold and unpleasant wriggle down her spine.

Shadow is very near, True Arica, warned Wish.

Within half an hour they found him near the edge of the forest, pawing at the frozen ground in an attempt to find some buried roots. She could feel the hunger gnawing at his insides, and sensed the terrible coldness that sank deep into his bones. Ribs strained against a dull, rough hide. Two bloodshot eyes rested on her face, then turned indifferently away. Breath rattled in lungs weary of the struggle, while muscles quivered with the effort of holding bones upright.

Go away, True One, he said. *And take your friend Wish with you. I want to be alone.*

His power was strong enough for her to feel it quite clearly, though he was obviously ill and half-starved. The last time she had seen him, Raden was riding on his back, and he had fallen just before Raden reached out to grab her. What had happened to him since then? Obviously nothing good. Anger burned inside of him as fiercely as ever, and she knew with terrible certainty that if he kept on this way he would die, probably within the next few months. Unicorns were never meant to live like this. They were creatures of light and joy, of freedom, and of wide-open spaces. Shadow had lived so long in his own bitter captivity that he had forgotten how to be what he was.

Arica slid to the ground and waited while Wish retreated to a discreet distance. The sun was slowly but inevitably cutting a pathway across the sky, and the lengthening shadows reminded her that they were running out of time. There was nothing she could do to prevent it — not even the magic of a unicorn could stop the rotating of a world.

She shivered as the wind plucked at her cloak and tossed her hair into her stinging eyes. Pushing it back with an impatient gesture, she stepped toward Shadow as he raised his head a second time. He didn't even glance her way as his horn swept through the air, throbbing with magic. He sent it crashing down upon the frozen ground. Dark magic spit in every direction, while the snow hissed and sizzled beneath his hooves. Then the cloud of moisture cleared to reveal a patch of soil scorched dry and a cluster of pale roots poking up like small, white bones.

Arica knelt and pulled at the roots with her fingers until some of them came free and others were exposed enough for his teeth to grasp. She didn't expect a thank-you and was pleasantly surprised when she got one. It wasn't much, really — only a brief flicker of gratitude that touched her mind for an instant and was gone — but it made her strangely happy and hopeful.

She waited patiently while he ate, and then, though he still ignored her, explained the situation as simply as she could.

"We need you, Shadow," she concluded. "And after this, no one will ever bother you again, if that's what you want. You can live out the rest of your life . . . undisturbed."

It took him so long to answer that she feared he wasn't listening, after all. But at last his ears flicked forward, and his head swung around until two dark eyes fixed on hers. She couldn't remember when she had ever seen so much pain.

Lately I have come to respect you a great deal, he

said. *But not enough for that.*

Arica hadn't known that he felt anything for her other than contempt, and it surprised her. He had changed in the last little while — more than she had thought possible. This was definitely a step in the right direction.

Clear thinking was what was needed now. Yet her wisdom had somehow vanished like a wisp of steam. She wanted to weep in frustration at Shadow's flat refusal to join his magic with the other unicorns'. She tried to rub the muddle from her aching head and then gave up and said the first thing that popped into her mind.

"May I touch you?" she asked.

He just stood there blinking at her as if she'd lost her mind, and at that moment, she thought he might be right. She moved close to him and stroked his nose and ran her fingers along his neck. His hide felt like sandpaper glued to wood. He flinched beneath her touch, but he didn't speak or pull away. That was something, at least. The anger was still there, but his torment was overwhelming the hate. Perhaps if she reminded him of the one thing in the world he still loved, she would be able to soften his heart to help her.

"Shadow," she said, hoping he didn't sense the desperation inside her. "Do you remember the ogre eye? Do you remember the vision that it showed you of the destruction of North Bundelag? Well, that's exactly what will happen tomorrow — if you don't join your magic with the other unicorns' and help me complete my spell."

My own kind drove me out, he said. The words rustled through her brain like dying leaves. *When I needed them most, they turned me away.*

"Forgive them, Shadow," she said. "Let your anger go before it consumes you. Hate and bitterness spread like poison, and in the end, they always destroy."

It wasn't fair, he insisted. *I want them to pay for what they've done.*

"You're right," she said. Inside she was frantic, but when she spoke, her voice was hardly more than a whisper. "You're right. It was terrible and unfair. But nothing you do can ever change that. Please put your anger aside and help me."

No, True One, he said. *That's the one thing I can never do.*

He was like a big, old ox stuck in a bog, and no matter how much you pushed and pulled and pried, he wouldn't budge. She turned and walked away. She'd gone a few dozen metres when she was stopped by a tree. Leaning her throbbing head against it, she fought back the tears.

With her eyes closed, she was more acutely aware of the sounds around her. A flock of sparrows twittered above her head. Branches creaked in the wind. Weapons clanged like hail on tin — obviously Grandmother's troops preparing for the battle. From some great distance, a single wolf cry rose into the air, thin and faint. And finally, hooves crunching over snow.

That must be Wish coming to find her. But she didn't want to face her friend and admit that she had failed. She didn't want to think about what would happen tomorrow, when that terrible army of humans poured across the river into North Bundelag like a plague of swarming insects and stole away everything she loved.

Lips of silk nuzzled their way across her cheek. Warm air stirred the hair along her neck and tickled in her ear. When she tried to pull away, the unicorn just followed her, the nibbling and blowing even more insistent. Finally Arica admitted she was beaten and glanced up to see two dark eyes staring sadly into hers.

It's not one person's fault, True Arica, Wish said. *It's just the way things are. Why do you blame yourself?*

"Stop trying to cheer me up," she grumped. "It's not going to work." But when she wrapped her arms around Wish's neck and pressed her face into that soft, sweet mane, she had to admit she felt a lot better. Letting go at last, she stepped back and prepared to mount.

Don't leave yet, said a voice in her head that wasn't Wish. *You started this conversation, so you have to finish it.*

Arica glanced over her shoulder at the unicorn that now stood a few metres behind her. She felt a jolt of hope — then clenched her teeth at the pain to come. This could only end in disappointment, and she didn't think she could bear any more of it.

"What is there left to say?" she asked, trying not to look at him. The way his lungs strained with the effort to breathe was like a fist in her gut. If only he didn't have to suffer so much.

You have an advantage . . . Shadow continued. Arica sensed that he was somewhat puzzled by her behaviour. *Didn't you notice that I'm weaker than I used to be? My power is waning. I'm no longer allied with the fairy Raden, which leaves me alone and vulnerable. You could easily overpower me with the combined magic of the unicorns and force me to complete your spell. Surely you're aware of these things.*

Arica stared back at him in stunned disbelief. Was he so corrupted by distrust and bitterness? She wiped her hand angrily across her eyes and willed back a fresh onset of tears. She had to explain this in a way that would make him understand her horror and dismay. She couldn't bear it if he went away still believing in a world where every word was a lie and every act of kindness a veiled threat.

"Listen to me, Shadow," she said. "Tomorrow morning the Fairy Queen will lead us into a war that we have little hope of winning. But she'll do it anyway, against impossible odds, because what we are fighting for is our freedom. Since coming to Bundelag, I've learned how important that is. So, even if I think the choice you are making is the wrong one, I could never take away your freedom to choose it. If I did, and then used you to fight for my own freedom and for that of my friends, I would be the worst kind of hypocrite and no longer fit to be called True One. Don't you see?"

She stopped, only because she had run out of breath and was feeling a little dizzy. What more could she say to him? He had already shown that he couldn't be convinced. Yet, if just a tiny amount of what she had said sank into that iron-plated skull of his, it would be worth the effort.

As Arica climbed onto Wish's back and nudged the unicorn into a gallop, she glanced back one last time to see Shadow staring after her, more perplexed than ever.

Chapter 12

It was a solemn throng of unicorns that met Arica and Wish on their return to Grandmother's camp. Connor rushed toward them, his face tense and anxious from waiting and wondering how things had turned out. Though he couldn't speak to the unicorns, Arica could tell that he sensed the mood of gloom hanging like a noxious cloud around them. He took one look at her face as she slid to the ground, and what little hope he was clinging to died in his eyes.

She sat on a log beside the fire and shivered beneath her cloak, cold and aching and sick at heart. Connor poured her a cup of hot soup from the pot and then hovered, discreetly silent, on the edge of her vision. She sipped it slowly, grateful for his thoughtfulness. Then she must have dozed off, for the next thing she knew she was snapping to awareness from Connor's shoulder, with Light's soft whisper tickling through her brain.

Wake up, True One, the stallion said.

She leaped to her feet just in time to see a cluster of unicorns part to make way for a much thinner, darker animal. Her heart, which had settled like a rock to the pit of her stomach, lurched sickeningly up to her throat and remained there, knocking wildly. The seconds dragged by like hours while she watched in disbelief as Shadow drew closer and closer to where she stood.

Evening had come, and the last rays of a dying sun transformed the still, silent unicorns around her into crystal statues touched with gold. In sad contrast, Shadow's poor, thin form was only a hodgepodge of skin and bones moving slowly over the snow toward her. He halted a few metres away, and she was hardly aware as Connor grabbed her arm to steady her.

True One, Shadow said. His thoughts came to her as gently as feathers brushing over silk. *When I refused your request, I felt your disappointment and it cut as deeply as my own. You could have simply taken what you wanted, but you gave me the gift of choice. I have come to trust you, though I fought long and hard* against it, and I want to return your gift. I've come to do as you asked. I've come to join my magic with yours and complete the spell.*

For a moment Arica was stunned speechless and just stood there looking at him and blinking foolishly.

"What is it?" Connor hissed in her ear. "What did he say?"

"He . . . he . . . " she stammered. Then with a rush of joy she flew across the snow, twisting her arms about Shadow's neck, and burying her face in his limp, stringy mane. He bore the embrace with a patience that did him credit, while Connor, who had already concluded the obvious, leaped around them and hooted with glee.

A ripple moved through the throng of unicorns and they drew closer, their silver manes glistening in the lengthening shadows, and their dark eyes shining with hope. They knew, and they were ready.

With the *Book of Fairies* on her lap, Arica prepared to work the spell. She was relieved to sense that a truce had been reached between Shadow and the other animals, and she was grateful for this brief moment of calm before the coming storm. The unicorns had come a long way in healing old hurts during these past few minutes — much farther than she had thought possible — but years of enmity and bitterness could not be erased easily.

Then with a rush of joy she flew across the snow, twisting her arms about Shadow's neck . . .

While the other animals kept their distance and eyed Shadow cautiously, Wish trotted right up to him and welcomed him into the group with a whinny and a nudge of her nose. The rush of warmth Arica felt for the little unicorn at that moment swelled to a painful lump in her throat. As Wish had matured, she hadn't lost her youthful innocence or her spontaneous, loving nature. At times like this, Arica hardly felt deserving of the friendship of this wonderful animal. Wish always made her want to try harder to be a better person.

"Thank you, Wish," she whispered and turned back to the task at hand.

The spell began — the same as before. She drew magic from the unicorns until it hummed in her head like a thousand bees and blazed, clean and blue, deep inside her bones. The power swelled, sweeping over her and through her like a molten river, and she continued to take it in, astonished that she could absorb so much magic without being harmed. As she took more and more of it inside her to form the spell of calling, she sensed what had been missing on her first attempt. Now there was a dark thread among the light. It was what Shadow's magic brought to her, and she knew that without it, the tapestry of her spell had been incomplete. Without it, the song inside of her had been only half sung.

Now there were drums and cymbals singing with the flutes, and as she sent the magic skyward, it seemed to fly on wings of sunlight and soar before the wind like a great, glittering kite. She called and felt the words speed straight and true to every corner of North Bundelag and into the ears of every creature that lived within its boundaries.

"Help us," she cried, over and over again. "Please help us. Come quickly, before it's too late."

Arica had no idea how long the spell held her in its fiery grasp or how many times she sent out her desperate plea, but at last it was over. She felt the magic drain suddenly from her bones, leaving her so weak and shaky that if Connor hadn't caught her, she'd have toppled nose first into a snowbank.

"Oh, wow," he said, as he settled her on a log beside the fire and tucked her cloak around her. "That was even better than the first time!"

She smiled wanly up at him and wondered if she would fall asleep the next instant or faint dead away from exhaustion. "What was it like?" she managed to whisper.

"Like fireworks exploding all over the place," he grinned. "Everything turned all blue and sparkly. You, the unicorns, and even me. Blue fire streaked into the sky like lightning, only it went up instead of down. The weird part was, there wasn't any sound. It was all so quiet and beautiful — like nothing I've ever seen. Too bad you missed it. Why did you close your eyes?"

"I didn't mean to," she said. "It just happened. The spell took a lot of concentration and effort — more than I've ever used before." She shivered, and Connor, after making certain she was all right, headed off into the trees for more wood to build up the fire.

Arica tucked her icy hands into a fold in her cloak. Despite the cold, she yawned hugely. What she wanted most right now was a hot bath, a huge pizza (any kind would do), and a soft, warm bed heaped with real feather pillows.

True One, said a voice, breaking into her happy daydream. She realized with surprise that her eyes had fallen shut again. She managed to pry them open, though it felt like someone had coated her lids with glue.

Shadow stood in front of her. Even in her muddled state, she could see that he had changed dramatically since the casting of the spell. The eyes that rested on her were clear and free of bitterness. Though he was still painfully thin, his coat had paled to pearly grey and glistened softly in the light of the fading sun. But most amazing — his dull, red horn had been transformed to pale gold.

All that power zapping around must have healed him, or at least helped to begin the process. A thrill of joy ran through her, and if she hadn't been so exhausted, she might have jumped up and hugged him for the second time this day. Instead she just sat there and grinned like a fool.

I'm leaving now, Shadow explained. *I've come to say goodbye. I need to be alone and think things through. So much has happened in such a short time. Light has offered me a place in Unicorn Valley if we win the war, and I might take him up on it. Or I might not. I've always been a loner, and I'm not sure I could change after all this time.

I'm disappointed in you, True One, he continued. *You didn't tell me that hate is a prison, and when you let go of it, you are free.*

Arica shook her head and tried to explain that this was precisely what she'd been telling him all along, but he had already disappeared. And when she attempted to call him back again, all that came out of her throat was a small, hardly audible squeak. Somehow she mustered up enough energy to crawl inside the tent. The last thing she remembered was Connor wrapping her in a blanket and telling her to rest well, that she deserved it, and not to worry because the unicorns were fine and he had everything under control.

Sometime during the night, she felt her grandmother's hand brush gently over her brow and tried to wake up, but without success. A while later, she heard Grandmother's voice mingled with Grandfather's and caught snatches of words that confused and yet intrigued her, as dream conversations so often do. She hoped Grandmother wasn't really here at all, but sleeping soundly in her tent nearby, getting what little rest she could before the coming battle.

" . . . proud of her," said Grandfather in her dream. "I knew . . . could do it."

"Our cause . . . nearly hopeless before last night," agreed Grandmother. " . . . only a little less hopeless now. Will they come, or . . . distance too great?"

Then Grandfather muttered something that Arica couldn't quite catch, and as she struggled to grasp at the fading tendrils of her dream, they dissolved away into the darkness.

She woke just before dawn to the sound of horns blaring in the distance and Connor shaking her by the arm. She groaned and sat up, her head pounding in time to the unwelcome serenade. Was this the after-effect of absorbing too much magic? It was an interesting thought, worth discussing at some later date. What she wouldn't do right now for a hot washcloth, and a plate heaped with eggs and buttered toast.

"It's time to get up," said Connor with a trace of anxiety in his voice. "I melted some snow in a pot to wash up with, but you'll have to hurry. I think those horns are a warning signal. The enemy must be getting ready to cross the river."

The day had come, then. Arica's heart thudded with a fear she couldn't quite suppress, but she did manage to muster up a weak smile.

"Thanks," she said. "But I'm disappointed. I was expecting breakfast in bed."

He grinned back. "Sorry, the kitchen is closed. You should grab some berries and biscuits though. Your grandmother said we need to keep up our strength."

"Grandmother was here?"

"Only for a minute," he admitted. "She looked like she hadn't slept all night, and she was in a terrible hurry."

It had been no dream, then. Arica's heart ached for her grandmother and the long, cold hours she must have spent waiting for dawn to come. But she didn't have to wait any more. The dreaded day had finally arrived.

Arica crawled out of the tent, splashed the steaming water over her face and hands, and wiped them with the rag Connor held out to her. Stuffing a few handfuls of dried berries into her cloak pocket, she peered around the clearing for Wish. There were unicorns everywhere, and she knew any one of them would carry her, but the only one she wanted was Wish.

Here I am, True Arica, said a voice inside her mind, and a moment later her friend trotted into view. Arica mounted, and with Connor astride Light and the mass of unicorns streaming behind, they turned their faces toward the south and headed off to fight a war.

Chapter 13

The battle horns sounded again just as Arica and Connor halted their unicorns on a small ridge overlooking the River of Songs. To the east, a pale sun peered reluctantly over the horizon, as if ashamed of what it saw below. From where they stood, they had a clear view of the surrounding valley. Arica's breath caught in her throat at the sight of so many soldiers. She couldn't see an end to them — spreading southward like a dark, ugly stain upon the silver land.

The two armies faced each other, still and silent as the naked trees and the frozen river that lay between them — waiting to begin. Arica couldn't see any ogres, though she knew exactly where they were hidden, and she marvelled at their ability to blend into the landscape without a trace. She saw Grandmother at the front of her army, cloaked in scarlet and gold — mounted on one of her grey stallions and with a jewelled sword glittering in her hand. Beside her, on the other grey stallion, sat Nue, proudly holding high the white flag of North Bundelag with its two gold, crescent moons. Arica had seen the flag fluttering in the wind above the fairy castle, and now she felt a thrill run through her to see that clean and simple symbol of peace. How strange to carry a white flag at the dawn of their greatest battle. How ironic that its bumbling bearer could become a hero.

Then the horns sounded for the third and final time, and the human army surged down the river-bank and onto the ice.

Arica pulled magic from the unicorns and sent it spinning out in a dizzy cloud of blue to settle over Grandmother and her army of fairies and elves. The light spread and thinned, until all that could be seen was a faint blue hue around each soldier's body. This was a different kind of magic than what she was used to, for she had to disperse it gradually and steadily, rather than in one great surge of power.

"I want to help," said Connor, as the first rush of human soldiers cleared the river and began swarming up the bank on their side. "I feel so useless just standing here and watching."

"You're not useless," Arica disagreed. "I need you."

"For what?"

"To guard our backs," she said. "If the unicorns get attacked from behind and have to use their magic to defend themselves, it would leave our army vulnerable to the bullets. I need you to warn me."

Connor grunted but didn't argue.

Arica could hear gunfire now — though, thankfully, not as much as she'd expected — mingled with shouting, the crunch of boots through snow, and the clang of sword against sword. Lost as she was in the swirl of the magic that surrounded her, she couldn't tell if the bedlam was lasting a few seconds or many minutes.

The sky was filled with birds before she noticed them. She had never seen so many different kinds all in one place, and they seemed to come from everywhere. There were huge black ravens like the ones that often followed Ega, razor-taloned hawks that screamed as they dived, and flocks of tiny silver sparrows. They peppered the sky with their bodies and fluttered and flapped around the heads of the invading army. The humans lashed out with their swords, distracted by the enormous feathered horde. A few of the braver birds landed on the soldiers' shoulders and began jabbing at their necks and ears.

Arica's joy at the sight was short-lived, however. She soon realized that the birds were no match for the humans, and the interruption in the forward advance would be a brief one.

A few minutes later, hope surged inside of her again, for the smaller land animals had arrived to join the conflict. Squirrels leaped onto pant legs. Porcupines bristled. Weasels darted underfoot, nipping and clawing. But what made her laugh out loud were the stinkrats, which looked like skunks and smelled even worse. They created havoc wherever they went, for as soon as the soldiers saw one coming, they panicked and dived out of its way.

The problem was that as soon as one soldier was gone, another arrived to take his place.

But the struggle wasn't over yet, and anything could happen. She saw the wolf Blackthorn lead his lean, red-eyed pack into the heart of the battle. She saw Shadow the unicorn repelling soldiers with the magic of his horn — alone still, but fighting for them all.

Her heart thudded with joy when she caught a glimpse of her own father riding alongside Grandmother and realized her call must have reached all the way to Earth. And what was this? She gasped in surprise as trolls swarmed out of the northern hills and joined with the ogres to hold back the invading army. Fairies, elves, animals, trolls, and ogres were fighting side by side — united at last.

And still the humans came.

As time wore on, Arica realized that this was as good as it was going to get. No more help was coming. They had all done their best, and it wasn't enough.

"There's just too many," Connor cried above the awful noise, echoing her own thoughts.

The magic she was taking from the unicorns was slowly waning, and when it was gone, the South would overpower the defenders in an instant and swarm east to the Fairy Village. Then they would storm the Fairy Queen's castle and install Raden on the throne, and all the magic in the grief-stricken land would die.

How could the *Book of Fairies* have been so wrong? The prophecy had foretold that she would save the land. Grandfather believed she could succeed, but she knew now that that was impossible. Despair encircled her heart in a crushing grip, and as she closed her eyes against the dreadful scene before her, a groan escaped and hung in the silence between her and her cousin like a sad "amen." The seconds dragged on to minutes, and the unicorns' magic drained away to a trickle and then was gone.

She was a coward, afraid to see, waiting with her eyes closed for Connor to tell her that the end had come.

"Look," he finally said, tugging on her arm. She opened her eyes reluctantly, puzzled by the excitement in his voice.

The sky was ablaze with red and orange kites.

Arica blinked and rubbed her eyes. No, the sky was ablaze with red and orange dragons. And there was a green one off to the right, and some blue ones approaching from the north, and even a brown one flecked with gold. They glided lazily through the pale morning, brilliant as jewels before the sun, with light glittering on their translucent wings and sparkling in their terrible golden eyes.

Only the huge black dragon dived. It must have known that a warning was all that was needed. Both armies paused in awe and watched the great dark beast plunge earthward, while the wind shrieked in its wings and birds scattered before it like dry leaves.

Just when Arica felt certain it would self-destruct, it levelled off above the ground and skimmed over the heads of the terrified human soldiers. Men howled and rolled as its claws raked the air over their tender scalps. A huge gout of fire erupted from its jaws, lighting up the battlefield that only seconds before had been crawling with men. Snow sizzled to vapour as the grass beneath it burned hot and red.

On the dragon's second pass, a third of the

human army turned tail and ran. More ground exploded into flame. By its fourth pass, most were in full retreat, while the prairie smoked and steamed behind them. The great beast swooped again and again, and those humans beyond the reach of the dragon's breath had only to glance at the dragon-filled sky to realize that the battle was over.

Arica slid from Wish's back, trembling with excitement, hardly believing what her own two eyes were telling her. Connor landed on the ground beside her, throwing his arms around her shoulders in an embrace she joyously returned. Breaking free, she planted a kiss on Wish's nose and another one on Light's, then caught sight of Grandmother in the distance, and took off down the hill after her, with Connor at her heels.

She was soon drowning in a sea of elves, Connor hopelessly lost somewhere behind her. As she wrestled her way through the riot of feet and flying elbows, she came upon a sight that made her stop short in astonishment, her heart banging beneath her ribs.

There stood her Grandfather — not the ghostly half-formed spectre she knew so well, but a real and solid man. His grey curls sprang out in tangled confusion, and his clothing hung in soiled tatters from his portly form. But good cheer sparkled in his eyes,

Both armies paused in awe and watched

the great dark beast plunge earthward.

and when she flew into his arms, the heart that beat against her ear was strong and steady and very much alive.

He laughed and threw her up into the air like he'd done when she was young, and caught her coming down. She laughed with him and tried not to topple over when he set her on her feet again. Girls who tame unicorns and call dragons into battle are meant to be steady on their feet at all times.

"What's happened to you, Grandfather?" she cried, thinking that this was a day full of surprises, each one better than the last.

Grandfather's eyebrows crinkled like two black caterpillars attempting to cross his face. "That vile, despicable woman!" he growled. "She turned me back to solid in the middle of the battle, and left me there without even a stick to defend myself with! That loathsome, wretched female! If I ever get my hands on her, I'll — "

"Who are you talking about, Grandfather?" she interrupted, fearing that if she didn't he would go on like this forever.

"My sworn enemy — Ega the Enchantress!" he bellowed.

At this, Arica's heart sank and her head whipped around. She stared up at the ridge where the unicorns had been only minutes before. Unfortunately, there were too many elves in the way to get a clear look. Without a word of explanation, she turned from Grandfather, elbowed her way through the happy throng, and dashed back up the hill.

She arrived just in time to see Ega dragging Wish into the forest by a rope.

Chapter 14

Arica cried out in horror and started after them, but Connor was there to grab her arm and hold her back.

"That's the payment Ega demanded," he explained, his face white with shock. "And Wish agreed. There's nothing we can do about it now."

"Just watch me!" said Arica and jerked her arm back. She had taken only a few steps when Light and Song stepped forward, blocking her way.

Let them go, True One, said Light, his thoughts laden with sorrow. *The bargain must be kept. Surely you know by now that we are creatures of honour. The troll would accept only a unicorn as payment, and my*

She arrived just in time to see Ega dragging Wish into the forest by a rope.

foal made the choice to go. *

Then Connor peered at her through his bottle-bottom glasses like a sad-eyed, pale-faced owl and took one deep, shuddering breath.

"Ega didn't waste any time," he said. "Your grandmother didn't even have the chance to talk to her." He sighed again. "I could be wrong, of course, but I believe she tricked us. This is what she wanted all along."

Arica slumped to the ground, too stunned and distraught to speak. For all her worry about what Ega would demand as payment, nothing could have prepared her for this. The thought of how Ega might harm Wish was more than Arica could bear. She buried her face in her arms and let the tears roll freely down her cheeks, not even caring to wipe them away.

"I'm so sorry," said Connor, patting her shoulder in a clumsy, boyish way. "I wish I could help."

She tried to thank him, but all that came out was a wet, gurgly gulp.

A moment later, someone large and strong plunked down beside her on a rock, and she found herself pulled against her grandfather's burly chest. She heard Connor blurt out an explanation and felt Grandfather's arms tighten in sympathy. After a few minutes he let go of her, dug a handkerchief out of his pocket, and began dabbing at her face.

"Nothing is as bad as it seems, dear girl," he said in a voice filled with tenderness. "I have my own score to settle with that Ega, and I won't rest until I find her. After that, we'll see what we can do." Grandfather patted her hand. "Shall we go and find your grandmother now? She'll get the surprise of her life when she sees me like this!"

Laughter rumbled in Grandfather's throat as he anticipated her grandmother's astonishment. He rose from the rock with a great amount of gasping and groaning. Connor rushed over to help, an adoring grin pasted on his silly face. Her cousin had idolized Grandfather right from the first moment they met, and this pitiful hero-worship thing was showing no sign of lessening.

"I'm all right, boy," Grandfather said, pushing Connor away. "I'm just not used to this body yet, that's all."

"I'd like to be alone for a minute," Arica said, as Grandfather held out his hand to her. "Do you mind going on without me?"

He grunted unhappily but finally nodded. "If that's what you want," he said, "but don't stay away too long." Then, with Connor trailing along in his wake, he clumped back down the hill and disappeared from sight.

Light and Song stood before her.

Goodbye, True One, they each said in turn.

Their dark eyes gazed on her one last time, filled with sadness and love. Then they headed northeast toward Unicorn Valley. Finally she was alone. For a while she just sat on the rock with her cloak wrapped around her and stared at the sky. The dragons were gone, and the smoke had cleared. Clouds drifted overhead like tiny white boats in a sea of crystal blue. Elves dashed past, calling out to one another in elated voices. The last remnants of the human army were specks in the distance.

The noonday sun gleamed down, promising more warmth than it had offered in a week. Snow sparkled like a silver blanket thrown across the prairie, and lay all white and glittering on the hills. Arica stood up, thrust her hand into her cloak pocket, and discovered the dried fruit she had placed there at dawn. She felt weak and ill and not the least bit hungry, but she nibbled on it anyway as she trudged along the ridge, down a narrow pathway, and through a clump of trees. At last she paused to rest beside the silent river.

Only footprints in the churned-up snow, broken branches and scattered bullet shells were left to remind her that the human soldiers had ever been here. She bent and clutched one of the tiny brass shells between her fingers, held it to the light, and studied it thoughtfully. The humans of South Bundelag had much to be ashamed of, with their hatred and their guns.

She tossed the shell carelessly over one shoulder, turned to head back the way she had just come, and looked up into the black, smouldering eyes of her Uncle Raden.

His sword was drawn, and when he made no immediate move toward her, Arica drew her own, knowing full well she stood no chance against him. His dark eyes gleamed with malice, and the words he spit from between his teeth were steeped in spite and bitterness.

"You've harassed me at every turn," he snarled, "and made my life miserable. You blew up my mine with magic, loosed my elves, turned Shadow against me, and stole the *Book of Fairies* from under my nose. But this time you've gone too far. The crown of North Bundelag should be mine, and you've driven away those who promised it to me. You've meddled in my affairs one too many times, little girl, and now you have no unicorn to protect you."

Arica stared back at him, so battle-weary and sorrowful over Wish that she couldn't muster up the energy to be afraid. The danger was as real as ever, for he was physically strong, but for the first time she was able to see him as he really was. And what she saw was that her uncle was not a brave and powerful man, as he wanted everyone to believe, but a bully who preyed on the weak and stole from the poor. An unexpected surge of pity welled up inside her as she spoke.

"Grandmother would welcome you back into the family," she said. "All you have to do is ask. She might even give you the throne some day, if you could prove that you were trustworthy. Why don't you come with me now and talk to her? Did you know that Grandfather is alive? I know he'd be thrilled to see you. He — "

For a moment Arica thought she had gotten through to him, for she saw a flicker of regret deep within his eyes. Then it was gone, squelched by all those years of heartlessness and greed.

"You've run out of time, little girl!" he cried.

His black cloak flapped about him as he lunged, and the sword that battered into hers nearly tore her arm from its socket. She stumbled backward. His second blow drove her to her knees and thundered in her head like a giant gong. She struggled to her feet just as he bore down upon her for the third, and likely final, time. Arica could barely lift her arm, and as she watched his sword plunge toward her breast, she could only think how heartbroken her loved ones would be when they found out what had happened.

The next instant, someone was beside her, and a hand closed over hers on the handle of her sword. Magic flowed into her — white-hot fairy magic that burned as it came, turning her skin to fire and her sword into a flaming, golden spear. Effortlessly, her arm swept upward and her glowing sword struck Raden's with a blast of power that wrenched his weapon from his clutch and sent it clattering across the ground.

Arica looked up into her father's eyes.

Before she could speak, he stepped in front of her, and the two brothers faced each other, only a stride apart. The air was thick with power and pent-up rage as they stared down the deafening silence. At last, her father broke the awful stillness with a steely warning that cut like a knife.

"Leave my wife and daughter alone," he said, "or you'll have me to deal with."

Arica had never seen her father so white-faced and angry, and it was quite likely that neither had Raden. The men's eyes locked and held while seconds crawled by like hours. Then Raden's gaze fell, and, with an oath, he turned and stomped away, his black cloak flapping around his boot tops.

The next thing Arica knew she was in her father's arms, hardly believing what had happened. When she finally pulled free from his embrace, Raden was no longer in sight, and Grandmother, Grandfather, Connor, and Connor's father (could it be?) were rushing over the snow toward them.

The reunion that followed was a joyous one, and when all the hugging and kissing and back-thumping was over, they stood apart and gazed at one another in relief, grateful that the war was won and that they were safe and together again. When all the inevitable questions were finally answered, Arica turned to her grandmother.

"There's something I don't understand," she said. "The trolls and dragons told us they wouldn't help, but in the end they came. It doesn't make sense. What made them change their minds?"

"You did," the Fairy Queen replied without hesitation. "Your call began a process of healing that will continue for years to come. Shadow has forgiven the other unicorns. Ega has released your Grandfather from a spell. The trolls have come down from the mountains to help the elves — an unheard-of event. The dragon-unicorn rift has begun to heal. And eventually there will be peace between North and South Bundelag. This is your magic gift, Arica. The unicorns can heal physical wounds in a wonderful way, but only your magic can take away bitterness and mend broken hearts."

Arica thought that over for a moment, then shook her head. "It does make some sense," she admitted, feeling a bit overwhelmed, "but how is it possible? I'm only a kid."

"But a very special one," added Grandfather, "just like I've always told you."

Arica turned back to Grandmother. "I have another question, but I promise it's the last one."

"Ask away," said Grandmother with a laugh.

"If you believed all this about my magic, why didn't you believe Connor and me about the prophecy in the *Book of Fairies?*"

Grandmother looked almost embarrassed. "To be honest with you, I never actually studied the prophecy. I haven't had much time for reading since you and Connor found the *Book of Fairies*. And I'm afraid that even if I had, I might still have had doubts. But perhaps it's just as well. It was your prophecy to fulfill, not mine. And you and Connor came through so beautifully — thank you."

After that Grandfather gave Arica an I-knew-all-along-you-could-do-it wink, and her father took her hand in his. Connor and Uncle Fred just stood and grinned at her.

"Now, thank you," she said to all of them. "I'm just glad I didn't let you down. I just wish . . ."

Answering her unspoken thought, Grandmother said, "Of course we shall do all we can on behalf of the unicorn. It is the very least we can do. Don't despair — you'll get Wish back if I have to recruit all of North Bundelag in the effort."

Then as everyone started to move away, Arica paused and gazed longingly toward the north one last time.

"I miss you, Wish. I'll think about you every day," she whispered.

Epilogue

The weeks dragged by, and all the while Arica's heart burned with an ache that never left her. When she looked up at the night sky, she imagined two moons instead of one and wondered what those two moons saw when they shone down on Wish.

Christmas came and went — the most sad and lonely one Arica had ever experienced. Her mother knew something was wrong, and tried to cheer her up with brightly wrapped gifts and all her favourite foods. Her father knew exactly what was wrong, and he tried even harder. She appreciated their love and concern, but there was nothing they could do to make up for her loss. There was nothing anyone could do.

Then one Saturday morning early in February, Mother insisted that she had moped around long enough, and today was the day to get her room back to normal. Arica groaned out a protest that was politely ignored, struggled up the stairs, and stood in the doorway of her room for a moment surveying the mess. Finally she gritted her teeth and dug in.

She was on her hands and knees sifting through a heap of books and old sweaters when she heard Wish's voice. It chimed sweet and clear like bells inside her head, and it was as real and true as anything she had ever heard.

Come quickly, True Arica, it said. *I am free.*

The atlas in Arica's hand thudded to the floor, already forgotten. Down the stairs she flew, hardly pausing as she grabbed her winter coat from the hook by the door. She had no time for boots or gloves and no need, for she was glowing with joy. She whipped open the door, leaped down the porch steps, and dashed past her father, who had just finished shovelling the sidewalk. Her eyes met his, and the look of relief on his face told her that he understood and approved of what she was doing.

The snow was too deep for a bike, so she had to make the trek to Grandmother's house on foot. Ten minutes later she was there, her fingers throbbing and her nose dripping and the icy air aching in her lungs. She thumped on the front door and was relieved when it opened to reveal the calm faces of her grandparents. They knew immediately, of course. Arica had been half-dead with grief for many weeks, and now she was alive again.

"How — ?" she gasped.

"A technicality!" Grandfather crowed. "That ship Ega offered you was stolen from elves, so she was never entitled to an ounce of payment."

It was a simple, bare answer, but it was enough. Arica's grandparents understood the need for speed. Grandmother took her hand, and together they hurried into the kitchen, dragged the rug away from its spot by the dishwasher, and stepped on the crack.

Arica felt herself drift gently downward through a spiral of darkness to land with a light bump on the cellar floor, still on her feet. Thinking of previous bone-jarring landings, she looked up at Grandmother and said, "You'll have to teach me how to do that sometime."

"Of course," Grandmother said and kissed her on the cheek. "Be sure to give Wish my love."

Then Arica opened the door in the cellar wall and dashed down the long underground tunnel, bursting out at last into a world of black, bare trees and grey skies and hilltops blanketed in white.

And there was Wish, with snowflakes on her ears and nose and laughter in her eyes.

Vicki Blum lives in High River, Alberta,
where she enjoys going for long walks
and looking at the mountains.
As an elementary-school librarian,
she loves working with books and doing
workshops with young writers.
A *Gathering of Unicorns* is the fifth and
final adventure in her best-selling
unicorn fantasy series.

When Arica falls through a crack in her grandmother's kitchen floor, she finds herself in a strange world of fairies, trolls, elves, and — best of all — unicorns. But the trolls and their evil master, Raden, take her prisoner, just as they have the unicorns. Fortunately, Arica discovers that she can hear the thoughts of the unicorns in a way that no one else in this world seems able to do.

With the help of Wish, a playful young unicorn, Arica sets out to free the captives — and discover the true reason she was brought to this magical land.

Wish Upon a Unicorn
by Vicki Blum
ISBN 0-590-51519-5
$4.99

The Shadow Unicorn
Vicki Blum
SCHOLASTIC

Through a half-open window the wind moans, as if in pain. *Help us, True One,* it seems to say, as it whispers through the leaves.

So begins Arica's return journey to the magical land of unicorns, fairies, and trolls. She arrives to find that the evil Raden is on the loose once again. With the help of a traitorous unicorn named Shadow, he has turned all the other unicorns to stone — all except Arica's friend, Wish.

Now it's up to Arica and Wish to stop them, and to bring the unicorns back to life.

The Shadow Unicorn
by Vicki Blum
ISBN 0-439-98706-7
$4.99

Arica has been summoned to North Bundelag and given a very important task: to cross over to South Bundelag, where cruel humans rule and unicorns dare not venture, and bring back the *Book of Fairies*. But this ancient treasure is in the hands of a greedy human merchant. And worse yet, the "horse" she's been given is actually the unicorn Shadow — her foe from an earlier battle.

Shadow says he is sorry for all he has done. But can Arica really trust him?

The Land Without Unicorns
by Vicki Blum
ISBN 0-439-98863-2
$4.99

Arica's evil uncle has poisoned her mother and escaped with her to Bundelag. There is only one hope: to find a rainbow flower, a magic ingredient in the cure from the *Book of Fairies*. Arica is prepared to fight dragons to get it, and is sure that her cousin Connor, the elves, and the unicorns will help her.

Then she learns of the unicorns' ancient promise, and with a sinking heart, Arica knows that their magic can't save her this time. At the last minute, will help come from an unexpected source?

The Promise of the Unicorn
by Vicki Blum
ISBN 0-439-98967-1
$5.99